The Spooky Mirror A Psychological Thriller

Marcelo Palacios

Published by INDEPENDENT PUBLISHER, 2024.

This is a work of fiction. Similarities to real people, places, or events are entirely coincidental.

THE SPOOKY MIRROR A PSYCHOLOGICAL THRILLER

First edition. October 7, 2024.

Copyright © 2024 Marcelo Palacios.

ISBN: 979-8227898760

Written by Marcelo Palacios.

Table of Contents

Chapter 1 1
Chapter 2 4
Chapter 3 6
Chapter 4 8
Chapter 5 10
Chapter 6 12
Chapter 7 14
Chapter 8 16
Chapter 9 18
Chapter 10 20
Chapter 11 22
Chapter 12 24
Chapter 13 26
Chapter 14 28
Chapter 15 30
Chapter 16 32
Chapter 17 34
Chapter 18 36
Chapter 19 38
Chapter 20 40
Chapter 21 42
Chapter 22 44
Chapter 23 46
Chapter 24 48
Chapter 25 50
Chapter 26 52
Chapter 27 54
Chapter 28 56
Chapter 29 58
Chapter 30 60
Chapter 31 62
Chapter 32 64
Chapter 33 66
Chapter 34 68
Chapter 35 70
Chapter 36 72
Chapter 37: New Horizons 74
Chapter 38 76
Chapter 39 78
Chapter 40 80
Chapter 41 82
Chapter 42 84

Chapter 1

Lisa Murphy was tired. The move to the old Victorian mansion had been more exhausting than I expected. Since morning, the rain had not stopped falling, a constant drizzle that seemed to accentuate the melancholy of the day. The mansion, with its imposing façade and time-worn architecture, had a somber beauty that both attracted and unsettled her. It was a new home, but the past seemed to be embedded in every corner.

He took off his soaked boots at the entrance and shook off his umbrella, trying to remove the water that had accumulated in the fabric. The room was filled with unpacked boxes, most of them stacked against the walls, waiting to be opened. Daniel, her husband, was in the office, trying to connect the new computer and get the Wi-Fi network working. Lisa knew he was just as tired as she was, but there was something in the air that made the task feel even heavier.

He decided that a little order in the attic could be a good distraction. Perhaps he would find something useful or, at least, he would manage to clear his mind of the endless routine of packing and unpacking. He climbed the creaking stairs and into the dusty space he hadn't seen since they arrived. The attic, with its sloping roof and exposed beams, was full of junk that even she didn't know where it had come from.

As she examined the old boxes and forgotten furniture, her hands came across an object covered by a blanket of gray powder. Lifting the blanket, he revealed an antique mirror, framed in an ornate bronze frame. Lisa stopped, shocked by the object's beauty and deterioration. The mirror had an air of lost elegance, as if it had witnessed generations of stories.

The frame was decorated with intricate patterns of leaves and flowers, and the surface of the mirror, although dirty, still reflected some light. Lisa reached over to clean it, using the edge of her T-shirt to rub the glass. As he did so, he noticed that the image that appeared was not completely clear. The reflection was blurry and distorted, as if something in the glass was altering reality.

The image the mirror returned to him was a dim version of the attic room, but there was something strange. The shadows seemed to move on their own, and the reflection in the mirror didn't quite match what Lisa saw. The feeling of discomfort increased in her stomach. The mirror seemed to have a life of its own, a mute enigma that kept asking him unanswered questions.

He decided he needed to investigate further. He carefully placed the mirror on the floor and began to examine the surroundings. He found no further clues as to its origin or history, but a sense of unease lingered. With every creak of the ground beneath his feet, he felt the mansion's past become more present.

She went down to the living room and met Daniel, who was already taking a break from his work. He was sitting on the couch, staring at his phone, trying to relax. Lisa came over and showed him the mirror.

"Look at what I found in the attic," he said, trying to sound enthusiastic despite his growing discomfort.

Daniel looked up, examining the mirror disinterestedly. "It's an old mirror." It looks like it could have been from someone important in the past.

Lisa nodded, but she couldn't help but feel that there was something else in that mirror. The uneasiness she had experienced when cleaning it did not leave her. "I think there's something strange about him. The reflection is not what it should be.

Daniel gave her a tired smile. "We'd better put it in the hall." If you don't like it there, we can always move it somewhere else.

Lisa accepted the suggestion. They passed the mirror into the hall and placed it against a wall. Although Daniel tried to cheer her up, Lisa's mind was still worried. The distorted vision of the mirror had left a mark on his mind, and he couldn't ignore the feeling that there was something more to that object.

That night, while Lisa and Daniel were having dinner, the sky darkened even more, and the rain lashed hard against the windows. Lisa was distracted, her thoughts swirling around the mirror and the strange sensation it provoked in her. Daniel noticed her lack of attention and looked at her with concern.

"All right?" "You seem worried," she asked.

Lisa smiled forcefully. "Just a little tired. It has been a long day.

"I know. Daniel got up and hugged her. "Try to relax. Tomorrow will be a new day.

Lisa tried to relax and enjoy dinner, but the mirror kept hovering in her mind. As they prepared to go to sleep, Lisa noticed that Daniel was more reserved than usual. Something about his behavior seemed strange, but he decided not to press him that night.

When she went to bed, Lisa couldn't stop thinking about the mirror. The distorted visions and shadows he had seen were echoing in his mind. When she finally settled into bed, she was plunged into a restless sleep, filled with disturbing images and a nagging feeling that something was very wrong.

The first nightmare came shortly after she fell asleep. In the dream, Lisa was in a dark and oppressive place. The mirror was there, hanging on an old, worn wall. As he approached, the glass began to crack, showing a desolate landscape inside. The woman trapped behind the glass looked at her with eyes full of despair. Lisa tried to touch the mirror, but an invisible force pushed her back, causing her to wake up with a start.

The rain kept pounding on the windows, and Lisa was drenched in cold sweat. He looked around, trying to calm his breathing. Daniel was by her side, asleep peacefully, oblivious to the nightmares that tormented her. Lisa got up and walked over to the hall, where the mirror stood silently. The distorted vision still lingered in her mind, and the image of the desperate woman kept tormenting her.

With a racing heart, Lisa walked over to the mirror and looked at it carefully. The reflected image was the same as he had seen before, but the sense of unease intensified. The shadows in the mirror seemed to move even more erratically, as if trying to communicate something to her.

He decided he needed answers. The story of the mansion and the mirror could not be so simple. Perhaps there was something deeper to discover. He spent the night researching in the house library, looking for any information that might shed light on the mirror's and the mansion's past.

The next morning, the sun had risen, but the storm was still leaving its marks. The sky was cloudy and the atmosphere was still heavy with moisture. Lisa decided to go to the local market to buy some cleaning supplies and hopefully find some information about the mansion's history. Daniel offered to stay home and continue with the task of unpacking.

As she walked through the aisles of the market, Lisa ran into her neighbor, Emily Turner. Emily was a middle-aged woman with a warm and friendly attitude. Lisa had met her briefly when they arrived, but she hadn't yet had a chance to talk in depth.

"Lisa!" What a surprise to see you here," Emily said with a smile.

"Hello, Emily. I'm just looking for some cleaning supplies. The move has been more complicated than I expected.

Emily nodded understandingly. "I completely understand. Moving into an old house always brings surprises. How's everything going in the mansion?

Lisa hesitated for a moment, considering whether she should mention the mirror. Finally, he decided to do it. "I found something strange in the attic. An antique mirror with a decorative frame. The image in the mirror is quite rare and it worries me a bit.

Emily's expression changed slightly, showing genuine interest. "That sounds intriguing. Old houses often have stories and secrets. Have you done some research on the history of the mansion?

Lisa nodded. "I have found some details, but nothing concrete. I thought you might know something else, given that you've lived in the area for a long time.

Emily was interested and offered to help. "Sure, I can help you investigate. The mansion has had several owners over the years. Perhaps there is some archive or document in the local historical archive that can shed more light on the mirror and its origin.

Lisa accepted the offer with gratitude. "That would be great. Can we meet later at the local library to do some research together?

Emily nodded. "Of course. I'm sure we'll find something interesting.

With a new hope of solving the mystery of the mirror, Lisa finished her shopping and returned home. Daniel was busy organizing the boxes, and Lisa mentioned her plan to investigate the mirror with Emily later.

The day progressed with a sense of expectation. Lisa and Emily found themselves in the local library, an old building with bookshelves full of books and historical documents. As they searched through the archives and records, Emily showed Lisa several documents about the history of the mansion.

After a few hours of research, they found a file containing information about the mirror. Apparently, the mirror had belonged to a prominent family that had lived in the mansion in the 19th century. The family had been known for its eccentric ways and dark secrets.

Lisa and Emily read the documents carefully. There were mentions of a tragic event related to the mirror, but the details were vague. The file spoke of unexplained disappearances and strange occurrences that had occurred in the mansion after the arrival of the mirror. Lisa felt a chill as she read the words. The mirror seemed to have a history as murky as its appearance.

With her heart pounding, Lisa thanked Emily for her help and returned home with the file in hand. The uneasiness he had felt when he found the mirror had increased, and now he felt that he was on the threshold of discovering something much greater than he had imagined.

When he got home, Daniel was waiting in the hallway. Lisa showed him the file and explained what she had discovered. Although Daniel was interested, his attitude was more reserved, and Lisa couldn't help but wonder if he knew something he wasn't telling her.

The night was unsettling again for Lisa. The mirror in the hall seemed to be watching her with its distorted reflection, and the shadows on the glass seemed more intense than before. The story of the mirror and the mansion was taking shape, and Lisa felt like she was about to discover something that would change her life forever.

Finally, he went to bed with his mind full of questions and the feeling that the past and the present were about to collide. The storm had ceased, but the storm in his mind was just beginning.

Chapter 2

Lisa Murphy was exhausted. The move to the old Victorian mansion had been far more exhausting than she had imagined. The day had been long, full of boxes to unpack and furniture to put up, and the incessant rain had only added an extra layer of melancholy and tiredness. The mansion, with its majestic but aged façade, had an imposing presence that seemed to amplify Lisa's fatigue.

Finally, after hours of work, Lisa climbed into bed, hoping that the night would offer her much-needed rest. Daniel, her husband, was already asleep next to her, his breathing regular and calm contrasting with the whirlwind of thoughts that Lisa couldn't avoid. The rain pounded insistently against the windows, creating a rhythmic sound that, far from being soothing, only increased the uneasiness in Lisa's heart.

The distorted reflection of the mirror, the recent discovery in the attic, was still present in his mind. The blurred image and shadows that seemed to move on their own had left him with a feeling of unease that he couldn't shake. Every time he closed his eyes, he saw the distorted outlines of the mirror and felt the presence of something dark and ancient lurking behind him.

Lisa turned on the bed, trying to find a comfortable position. Every creak of the house seemed amplified in the silence of the night, and the sound of rain had become a constant and annoying accompaniment. His mind was filled with images of the mansion and the mirror, and his uneasiness became more and more palpable. She couldn't stop thinking about the nightmares she'd had the night before, and the feeling that the mirror was a door to something dark and unknown didn't leave her.

Finally, Lisa couldn't take the insomnia anymore. She got out of bed carefully so as not to wake Daniel, and went to the hall where the mirror was placed. The house was in darkness, and the only light came from the floor lamp he had placed near the mirror. The dim glow of the lamp cast shadows on the walls and floor, creating an unsettling atmosphere.

Lisa walked over to the mirror, her heart pounding as she watched him. The bronze frame was covered in dust, and the intricate decorations of leaves and flowers seemed to come alive in the dim light. He moved closer, wiping the dust with the edge of his shirt. The mirror showed the same distorted reflection he had seen before, but now, under the light of the lamp, the shadows on the glass seemed to move even more erratically.

Restlessness took hold of her as she stared at the mirror. The reflection of the lobby room seemed to distort and change shape, and the shadows on the glass seemed to dance eerily. Lisa tried to ignore the feeling of discomfort that invaded her and focused on the reflection. He looked at the details of the room in the mirror: the furniture, the boxes not yet unpacked, and the objects scattered on the floor. Everything seemed right, but there was something about the way the mirror reflected it that didn't quite fit.

Suddenly, Lisa saw a movement in the reflection that didn't correspond to reality. A dark shadow seemed to glide through the glass, and a feeling of cold ran down his spine. Lisa blinked, and the shadow disappeared, but the feeling of unease persisted. He decided he needed to be distracted and headed to the local library to look up information about the history of the mansion and the mirror.

Arriving at the library, he found the quiet atmosphere of an old building, filled with bookshelves full of books and documents. The warm light from the lamps contrasted with the cold and humidity of the night. Lisa began to go through the mansion's historical archives, looking for any details that might shed light on the mirror and its origin.

While going through the documents, he came across a file containing information about the original family that had owned the mansion. The archive spoke of the family as prominent people in the community, known for their customs and opulent lifestyle. However, he also mentioned that there had been several disappearances and strange happenings related to the mansion over the years. Lisa was intrigued by the connection between these events and the mirror, and decided she needed to investigate further.

Upon returning to the mansion, Lisa felt a growing sense of urgency. The mirror and the history of the mansion were intertwined in a way that he couldn't ignore. As he walked through the dark halls of the house, the sound of rain and the creaking of floorboards created an unsettling atmosphere. Lisa felt watched, as if the mansion itself was waiting for her to discover its secrets.

He went back to the lobby and looked at the mirror, now with a new perspective. The information he had found in the library seemed to indicate that the mirror might have a connection to the strange happenings in the mansion. Lisa wondered if there was more to the mirror than just an antique piece of décor.

With her heart racing, Lisa decided that she should examine the mirror more thoroughly. He approached the object and began looking for any markings or inscriptions on the frame that might offer further clues. As he did so, he noticed something he hadn't seen before: a small metal plate at the bottom of the frame, partially hidden by dust and wear. The plaque was engraved with a name and date, but the words were difficult to read due to the condition of the metal.

Lisa wiped the plate carefully, trying to decipher the text. Finally, he managed to read the name "Margaret Whitmore" and a date that seemed to indicate the year in which the mirror had been made. The information seemed to fit with what he had found in the historical archives: Margaret Whitmore was the name of the wife of the mansion's first owner, and the date coincided with the period when the family had lived in the house.

Lisa was intrigued by the connection between the mirror and Margaret Whitmore. The family's history and the disappearances related to the mansion seemed to be linked to the mirror more deeply than I had imagined. The sense of unease intensified, and Lisa felt like she was about to discover something important.

He decided that he should continue to investigate and seek more details about Margaret Whitmore and her relationship with the mirror. The next day promised to be long, but Lisa was determined to unravel the secrets the mansion held. The rain kept falling, and the sound of drops hitting the windows had become a constant in his life, a reminder that the secrets of the past were waiting to be revealed.

He returned to bed with a mixture of exhaustion and excitement. Daniel was still asleep next to her, oblivious to the uneasiness that had invaded Lisa. As he settled under the covers, his mind kept spinning around the mirror and the story he was beginning to discover. She knew that the next day would be crucial in solving the mystery and finding answers to the questions that plagued her.

With her mind full of thoughts and the feeling that she was about to hit a big reveal, Lisa finally managed to close her eyes and fall into a restless sleep. The rain continued its constant pounding on the windows, and the mirror in the hall seemed to continue to watch her, waiting for the moment when the secrets of the past would be revealed.

The chapter closed with the promise of more discoveries and the expectation that the night, with its shadows and mysteries, was far from over.

Chapter 3

Lisa woke up early, before the sun began to illuminate the old mansion. He had spent a restless night, plagued by haunting dreams and memories of the haunting visit to the library. Although the constant sound of the rain had been partly comforting, the weight of the secrets and mysteries surrounding the mirror did not let her rest.

She got out of bed carefully, trying not to wake Daniel, who was still sleeping soundly. Lisa dressed quickly and went to the lobby to take a look at the mirror. The object seemed to wait patiently, its presence imposing and its bronze frame adorned with intricate detail.

While eating breakfast, Lisa mentally went over the steps she needed to take to investigate more about the mirror and the history of the mansion. He decided that the first step would be to consult the documents he had found in the library and seek more information about Margaret Whitmore and her family. The connection between the mirror and the strange happenings in the mansion seemed to be the common thread of the story I needed to unravel.

After a quick breakfast, Lisa prepared for another day of research. She made her way to the local library, where she met Emily Turner, who had shown interest in helping her with the research. Emily was ready to work and was enthusiastic about exploring the historical records further.

Together, Lisa and Emily went through the files again, looking for any additional details about Margaret Whitmore and the Whitmore family. They found several documents that spoke of the family, but most of them were general descriptions about their life and social status. However, one file in particular caught Lisa's attention: an old diary that appeared to belong to Margaret Whitmore.

The diary was bound in worn leather and had a delicate appearance. Lisa opened it carefully, trying not to damage the fragile pages. The first entries in the diary described the daily life of Margaret and her family, their social events and their concerns. However, as Lisa read more, she noticed that the tone of the diary changed. The last pages were filled with notes about strange happenings and growing concerns.

Margaret had written about feelings of being watched, unexplained noises in the house, and a general sense of unease. In one of the most disturbing entrances, Margaret mentioned a "distorted reflection" in the mirror that had been placed in the hall of the mansion. The descriptions were vaguely similar to the sensations Lisa had experienced when looking at the mirror.

Lisa and Emily continued to go through the diary, finding more details about Margaret's mental state and her growing despair. Margaret had tried to seek help, but her efforts seemed fruitless. By the end of the diary, the writing became more disorganized and erratic, with mentions of dark visions and presences that I could not explain.

The discovery of the diary left Lisa and Emily with a sense of urgency. The connection between the mirror and the strange happenings in the mansion seemed increasingly clear, and Lisa felt like she was about to unveil something important. He decided that he should speak to the local historian, Dr. Samuel Greene, who might have more information about the events that had occurred at the mansion.

Dr. Greene was known for his knowledge of local history and the investigation of paranormal phenomena. Lisa and Emily headed to their office, a small brick building near the city center. Dr. Greene was an older man, with gray hair and a kind but serious demeanor. He greeted Lisa and Emily with interest when they told them about their findings.

After hearing Lisa's story and reading the diary notes, Dr. Greene was intrigued. He explained that the Whitmore mansion had been the scene of several bizarre events over the years, including rumors of disappearances and apparitions. Although many of the events were considered urban legends, Dr. Greene did not rule out the possibility that there was some truth to the stories.

"The mirror is a key element in this story," said Dr. Greene. —Ancient mirrors were often associated with esoteric beliefs and practices. In the past, it was thought that mirrors could reflect more than just images; they were attributed powers to capture souls or open portals to other worlds.

Lisa listened intently, feeling the pieces of the puzzle begin to fall into place. The idea that the mirror might be related to esoteric practices and paranormal phenomena fit with the unsettling sensations I had experienced. He decided that he should further investigate the mirror's past and its possible connection to esoteric practices.

Dr. Greene also suggested that Lisa and Emily investigate the local church archive. There was a possibility that there were records about rituals or events related to the mansion and the mirror. Lisa and Emily thanked Dr. Greene for his help and headed to the church, which was located on a nearby hill.

The church was an ancient and majestic building, with colorful stained glass windows and an atmosphere of solemnity. They met with the parish priest, Father Jonathan, who showed them the church's archive. Lisa and Emily began to go through the documents, looking for any mention of the Whitmore mansion or esoteric practices.

They found several documents related to the history of the church, but they also discovered a number of ancient records that mentioned rituals and practices that were performed in the region. Although most of the records were related to religion and religious ceremonies, there were some notes about darker and more secret rituals being performed in the community.

Lisa felt a chill as she read about the esoteric practices and dark rituals that had taken place in the region. The connection between these rituals and the mirror seemed increasingly apparent. He decided that he should investigate more about the rituals and their possible connections to the strange events in the mansion.

Upon returning to the mansion, Lisa was determined to unravel the secrets of the mirror and the mansion. I knew the road ahead would be long and complicated, but I was ready to face whatever came my way. Night had come, and the sound of rain was still a constant reminder that the secrets of the past were waiting to be revealed.

Lisa made her way to the hallway, where the mirror seemed to be watching her in silence. With renewed determination, he prepared to continue his investigation and uncover the truth behind the mirror and the dark secrets of the mansion. The connection between the past and the present was becoming clearer, and Lisa was ready to face the challenges that lay ahead.

Chapter 4

Lisa Murphy woke up before dawn, with a sense of determination and anxiety. The discovery of Margaret Whitmore's diary and the revelations of Dr. Greene and Father Jonathan had added a new layer of urgency to her investigation. He knew that the mirror and the mysteries of the mansion were more intertwined than he had imagined, and he felt that he must act quickly to unravel the truth.

After a quick breakfast, Lisa decided that the next step would be to examine the mansion's attic for additional clues. There was a chance that he would find something more related to the mirror or the Whitmore family. The attic, which was still littered with boxes and antique furniture, seemed like a place prone to hiding secrets.

He climbed into the attic with a flashlight in hand, illuminating the dark space with his dim light. The air in the attic was heavy and dusty, and the smell of old wood and dampness filled his senses. While going through the boxes and furniture, Lisa came across several pieces of antique furniture and discarded objects, but nothing that seemed directly related to the mirror.

Finally, he found a small, dusty box in a corner of the attic. The box was locked with a rusty lock, but Lisa managed to open it carefully. Inside the box were several antique objects, including documents, black-and-white photographs, and a number of letters. Lisa began to go through the contents of the box, looking for any clues that might be related to the Whitmore family.

Among the letters and documents, Lisa found a series of photographs that caught her attention. The images showed the Whitmore family on several occasions, and on some of them, the antique mirror was present in the background. The photographs offered a glimpse into the family's daily lives, and Lisa observed details that seemed to match the descriptions in Margaret's diary.

In one of the photographs, Lisa noticed a disturbing detail: the mirror was surrounded by candles and strange symbols. The image seemed to indicate that the mirror had been used in some kind of ritual or ceremony. The connection between the mirror and esoteric practices seemed increasingly apparent.

Lisa also found a letter that appeared to be from Margaret Whitmore. The letter was written in an anguished tone and described the growing sense of despair and fear Margaret felt. In the letter, Margaret spoke of a "dark pact" and the need to find a way to break it. The letter was signed with the date on which the mirror had been placed in the mansion.

The contents of the letter left Lisa with a sense of unease. The idea of a dark pact and the need to break it fit with the feelings of discomfort I had experienced. Lisa wondered what kind of pact Margaret had made and how it might be related to the strange events at the mansion.

With a racing heart, Lisa decided that she should continue investigating. The connection between the mirror, the dark pact, and the events in the mansion seemed to be taking shape, and Lisa was determined to uncover the truth. He headed to the local library to revisit the historical archives and seek more information about the dark pact mentioned in the letter.

When he arrived at the library, he found Emily Turner waiting. Emily had been researching esoteric practices and dark rituals, and was ready to help Lisa with her research. Together, they went through the files and documents for any mention of the dark covenant or rituals related to the mirror.

After several hours of research, they found an ancient document that spoke of an esoteric ritual performed in the region during the 19th century. The document described a ritual involving an ancient mirror and a pact with dark forces. The ritual was aimed at gaining power or knowledge in exchange for a sacrifice, and the mirror was considered a means of connecting with supernatural entities.

The document provided details about the ritual, including the symbols and ceremonies that took place. Lisa and Emily compared the information with the photographs and documents they had found in the attic, and the coincidences were disturbing. The mirror in the Whitmore mansion appeared to have been used in a dark ritual involving a pact with supernatural forces.

Lisa felt a chill as she considered the possibility that the mirror was linked to esoteric practices and a dark pact. The idea that the mansion and the mirror could be related to supernatural forces was unsettling, but Lisa was determined to uncover the truth.

As they continued to investigate, Lisa and Emily received a call from Daniel. Daniel had found something unusual in the basement of the mansion and wanted Lisa to come and see him. Lisa and Emily quickly made their way to the mansion, hoping that Daniel's finding might provide more insight into the mysteries surrounding the house.

When they arrived in the basement, they found Daniel going through a series of boxes and old objects. Among the objects, there was a wooden box that looked especially old. Daniel had found a set of documents and objects inside the box, and some of them seemed to be related to the mirror and the strange events in the mansion.

Lisa and Emily checked the contents of the box carefully. They found several documents, including old letters and records, that spoke of the Whitmore family and the events that had occurred at the mansion. They also found a number of esoteric objects, including amulets and symbols that appeared to be related to the dark ritual mentioned in the documents.

Among the documents, Lisa found a letter written by a member of the Whitmore family. The letter described an attempt to break the dark covenant and free themselves from the supernatural forces that had been summoned. The family member had written about a counterposition ritual that might be necessary to break the covenant and reverse the effects of the original ritual.

The contents of the letter provided a new perspective on the dark covenant and the mirror. Lisa felt that she was getting closer to a clearer understanding of the events that had occurred in the mansion. The need to perform a ritual of counterposition seemed to be a crucial part of the story and could be the key to solving the mystery of the mirror.

With the information she had found, Lisa decided that she should prepare the counterposition ritual mentioned in the letter. The thought of facing supernatural forces and breaking the dark pact was terrifying, but Lisa was willing to do whatever it took to solve the mystery and protect her family.

That night, Lisa made her way to the lobby, where the mirror waited in silence. With renewed determination and the documents and objects she had found, Lisa began to prepare the ritual of opposition. The atmosphere in the mansion was tense and fraught with anticipation, and the sound of rain was still a constant reminder that the secrets of the past were waiting to be revealed.

While preparing the ritual, Lisa felt a mixture of fear and hope. I knew I was about to face something dark and unknown, but I also felt like I was taking a crucial step toward the truth. With each step she took, the connection between past and present became clearer, and Lisa was ready to face the challenges ahead.

Chapter 5

The air in the mansion was charged with palpable tension as Lisa Murphy prepared the ritual of counterposition. The atmosphere was gloomy, illuminated only by the faint light of the candles he had arranged around the mirror. The constant sound of rain pounding on the windows of the mansion created an ominous backdrop that intensified the sense of unease. Lisa had carefully followed the instructions on the document and the letter found in the basement, arranging the symbols and esoteric amulets according to the requirements of the ritual.

As she laid out the final details, Lisa recalled the conversation she had had with Emily and Daniel about the ritual. Daniel, though concerned for Lisa's safety, had decided to support her decision and had offered to help her in any way he could. Emily, equally committed to the investigation, had arranged to supervise and assist during the ritual. Both were prepared to face the unknown with Lisa.

The vestibule, where the mirror had been placed, was the central place of the ritual. Lisa had chosen this place not only because it was the place where she had found the mirror, but because she felt that the energy of the place was deeply connected to the events of the past. The mansion had been plunged into silence and gloom, as if it were also waiting for the denouement of the mysteries that had accumulated over the years.

The mirror, with its bronze frame and polished surface, reflected the light of the candles, creating a play of shadows that danced on the walls. Lisa felt that the mirror had a presence of its own, an entity that observed and waited. He took a deep breath and began to recite the words of the ritual in a low voice, following the instructions of the ancient document.

The first part of the ritual involved drawing a circle around the mirror using a special powder that Lisa had prepared with esoteric ingredients. As Lisa carefully traced the circle, the atmosphere seemed to become denser, and the temperature in the room dropped slightly. Daniel and Emily watched silently, their faces tense as Lisa went through the ritual.

Once the circle was complete, Lisa placed the amulets and symbols around the mirror, following the pattern described in the document. Each symbol was designed to protect and focus energy during the ritual. Lisa lit the candles and began placing small fragments of crystals and aromatic essences at the specific points around the circle.

While Lisa made these preparations, Daniel and Emily took it upon themselves to keep watch. They knew that the ritual could attract dark energies or presences, and they were prepared to intervene if necessary. The mansion was shrouded in expectant silence, and the sound of rain was still a constant accompaniment.

With the circle ready and the symbols in place, Lisa began the second part of the ritual. He recited a series of words in an ancient language that he had found in the documents. The words were unintelligible to her, but they knew they were critical to the success of the ritual. Lisa felt a growing sense of power and connection to the forces that were about to be summoned.

Suddenly, a gust of cold wind swept through the room, and the candles flickered. The mirror began to show an unusual glow, and the shadows on the glass seemed to move erratically. Lisa felt a wave of energy envelop her, and the atmosphere in the lobby became even more tense. The words of the ritual seemed to echo in the air, amplified by the presence of the mirror.

As the ritual progressed, Lisa began to notice changes in the reflection of the mirror. The surface of the glass seemed to distort, showing glimpses of scenes from the past. Images of the Whitmore family, of ancient events and of unsettling moments appeared and disappeared in the reflection. Lisa was absorbed in the visions, trying to keep her focus on the ritual.

At a crucial moment, the mirror showed a particularly disturbing image: a dark, shadowy figure that seemed to move toward the edge of the glass. The figure had an oppressive, malevolent presence, and Lisa felt a chill run through her body. He knew he had to continue with the ritual despite the growing sense of danger.

He recited the final words of the ritual with determination, focusing his intention on breaking the dark pact and freeing the mansion from the forces that had been summoned. The energy in the room reached a climax, and the mirror began to show an intense glow. The shadows on the crystal slowly dissolved, and the dark figure disappeared.

When Lisa finished the ritual, the atmosphere in the lobby changed. The atmosphere became lighter, and the cold that had invaded the room disappeared. The candles flickered and then went out, and the mirror returned to showing a normal reflection, without the disturbing distortions of before. Lisa felt a deep sense of relief, but also a sense of exhaustion. The ritual had been successful, but the cost in terms of energy and concentration had been high.

Daniel and Emily reached out to Lisa, offering their support and concern. Daniel hugged Lisa, worried about her condition. Emily offered words of encouragement and helped clean up the ritual area. Lisa thanked them for their support and explained what she had experienced during the ritual.

Although the mirror seemed to have returned to its normal state, Lisa knew that the danger was not over. The events of the past and the dark forces that had been present in the mansion might have left traces or consequences that he didn't yet understand. He decided that he should continue to investigate and seek more answers about the history of the mansion and the Whitmore family.

The night continued with a renewed sense of calm in the mansion. The rain had subsided, and the sound of drops falling on the roof had become a distant echo. Lisa, Daniel, and Emily gathered in the living room, exhausted but relieved. They knew the road ahead still had challenges, but they were determined to face whatever came their way.

The ritual had marked a turning point in Lisa's research, and the reflection in the mirror seemed to have regained its normal appearance. However, Lisa felt that the mirror still held secrets and that its connection to the events of the past was far from fully revealed. With renewed determination, Lisa prepared to continue her search for answers and face the mysteries that still remained to be solved.

Chapter 6

The next morning arrived with a cool and calm atmosphere, in contrast to the intensity of the night before. Lisa Murphy, though exhausted by the ritual, woke up with a sense of renewed determination. The success of the ritual had provided temporary relief, but Lisa knew that many questions remained unanswered. The connection between the mirror, the dark pact, and the events in the mansion remained enigmatic.

She prepared for a new day of investigation, determined to delve deeper into the history of the Whitmore family and the mysterious events that had taken place at the mansion. Daniel and Emily were also committed to finding answers and offered to accompany her in her efforts.

Before starting, Lisa checked the contents of the box she had found in the basement. Apart from the letters and documents he had already examined, there was a small notebook that appeared to have been written by a member of the Whitmore family. The notebook was full of notes about events and observations, and Lisa hoped it could provide more useful information.

The notebook was filled with detailed records about the family's day-to-day life and their interactions with the mansion. However, some pages were marked with strange symbols and notes about unusual events. Lisa focused on the sections that mentioned the mirror and esoteric rituals. He found a particularly intriguing entry that told of a series of encounters with a mysterious individual.

The entry described a man who visited the mansion in secret and seemed to have in-depth knowledge about esoteric practices. The man had made several recommendations on how to handle the mirror and protect himself from dark forces. The entry also mentioned that the man had left behind an object that could be key to understanding the mystery.

Lisa decided that she should investigate more about this individual and the object she had left behind. The entry in the notebook provided a vague description of the man and a mention that he had left an object in a specific place in the mansion. Lisa made her way to the lobby, where the mirror was located, and began searching for any clues about the aforementioned object.

While checking the area, Emily and Daniel took it upon themselves to investigate other places in the mansion. Emily scoured the library's archives for additional information about the mysterious visitor, while Daniel scanned the basement for clues to the object left behind.

Lisa scanned the lobby closely, looking for any objects or signs that might be related to the mysterious visitor. After a thorough inspection, Lisa found a small box hidden behind one of the decorative columns in the lobby. The box was similar to the one I had found in the attic, but it seemed to be in better condition.

Cautiously, Lisa opened the box and discovered a collection of objects and documents. Among them, he found a series of esoteric amulets, a small antique key, and a handwritten note. The note was addressed to Margaret Whitmore and contained instructions on how to use the amulets to protect oneself from dark forces. It also mentioned that the key could open a secret compartment in the mansion.

Lisa felt a mixture of excitement and concern when she found the note. Information about the amulets and key could provide important answers about the mystery of the mirror and the dark covenant. He decided that he must find the secret compartment mentioned in the note.

Meanwhile, Emily had found an ancient record in the library that spoke about the mysterious visitor. The record provided more details about the man, including his name: Jonathan Blackwood. Blackwood had been an expert in esotericism and had been known for his knowledge of dark rituals and practices. The information in the log suggested that Blackwood had had a significant influence on the events that had occurred at the mansion.

With the information she had found, Lisa decided that she should investigate more about Jonathan Blackwood and his connection to the Whitmore family. The presence of the amulets and the key indicated that Blackwood had played a crucial role in the events surrounding the mirror.

Lisa and Emily were reunited with Daniel, who had also found some extra documents in the basement. The documents spoke of the history of the mansion and mentioned several strange events, including the dark rituals that had taken place. Daniel had found references to a "shadow book" that contained information about rituals and how to counter them.

With the information gathered, Lisa, Daniel, and Emily decided that the next step would be to search for the secret compartment mentioned in the note. The mansion was full of hidden hiding places and passageways, and the compartment could contain key information to solve the mystery.

They made their way to the lobby, where Lisa and Daniel began looking for a place that could hide the secret compartment. The small key found in the box seemed to be the right instrument to open it. After a thorough search, they found a door hidden in one of the walls of the lobby. The door was covered by a decorative panel that slid to the side to reveal a hidden space.

Inside the secret compartment, they found a number of ancient documents and a leather-bound book. The book appeared to be the "book of shadows" mentioned in the documents found by Daniel. Lisa and Emily reviewed the contents of the book, which was filled with instructions on esoteric rituals and practices. The book provided details on how to perform rituals of protection and counter dark forces.

While going through the book, Lisa and Emily found a chapter that seemed to offer instructions on how to break a dark pact. The instructions were detailed and required several ingredients and specific rituals. Lisa felt a sense of relief to discover that the book contained valuable information to solve the mystery.

The information in the book and in the documents helped clarify the connection between the mirror, the dark covenant, and the events at the mansion. Lisa realized that the pact had been made by a member of the Whitmore family in a desperate attempt to gain power and knowledge. The pact had involved a dark ritual and had left a mark on the mansion and on the mirror.

With the new information, Lisa, Daniel, and Emily prepared to carry out the next step in the investigation. They knew they needed to be cautious and prepared to face any challenges that might arise. The mansion was still a place fraught with mystery and danger, and the path to the truth was full of obstacles.

That night, as the rain continued to fall outside, Lisa sat in the lobby with the shadow book and documents beside her. She was determined to unravel the secrets of the mirror and the mansion, and she was ready to face whatever came her way. The reflection in the mirror, now seemingly normal, seemed to be watching her in silence, as if it were also waiting for the denouement of the mysteries that had been hidden for so long.

Chapter 7

The next day dawned with a thick fog enveloping the mansion, creating an even more mysterious and oppressive atmosphere. Lisa Murphy, Daniel, and Emily had gathered in the library, determined to dig deeper into the investigation with the new information they had discovered. The shadow book and the documents found in the secret compartment offered an opportunity to solve the riddles surrounding the mirror and the dark pact.

As the group prepared to work, Lisa was encouraged by the progress they had made, but she was also aware that the challenges they faced could be even more complex than they expected. The fog that covered the mansion seemed to be a reflection of the confusion and mystery that still surrounded their search.

Emily had taken the time to review the details of the book of shadows, writing down the ingredients and rituals needed to counter the dark pact. Lisa had been reading the old documents for clues about the Whitmore family's history and any additional details that might be relevant to her investigation. Daniel, meanwhile, was researching Jonathan Blackwood's role in the mansion's history and his connection to the dark covenant.

The book of shadows contained a number of esoteric rituals and practices, some of which seemed to be directly related to the mirror and the covenant. The information about the counter-ritual was detailed and complex, requiring several ingredients and specific steps to carry out. Emily was particularly interested in the protective ritual described in the book and how it could be applied to protect Lisa and the group during the investigation.

While Lisa was going through the documents, she found a reference to an important event in the history of the mansion. The document spoke of a ceremony performed by the Whitmore family that appeared to be linked to the dark covenant. The ceremony had taken place at a specific location in the mansion, and the document included a detailed description of the venue and the rituals that took place.

Lisa decided that they should investigate the place mentioned in the document. The site appeared to be located in a secluded section of the mansion, and the document stated that it was a secret basement that had been used for esoteric rituals. With the information from the document in hand, the group prepared to explore this new area of the mansion.

They made their way to the area mentioned in the document, which was located in a hidden part of the basement. The passage was narrow and dark, and the air was permeated with a musty and musty smell. The fog outside seemed to have infiltrated the basement, creating an even more gloomy atmosphere.

Lisa, Daniel, and Emily followed the passageway, using flashlights to light their way. After a short tour, they came to an ancient iron gate that seemed to have been sealed for a long time. The door was covered in dust and cobwebs, and the lock looked rusty. With the antique key found in the secret compartment, Lisa tried to open the door.

The key fit perfectly into the lock, and with a careful turn, the door opened with a squeak. On the other side of the door was a large, empty room, with stone walls and a dusty floor. In the center of the room was an ancient altar, with esoteric symbols carved into the stone.

Lisa approached the altar cautiously, examining the symbols and details of the place. The altar seemed to be aligned with the rituals described in the shadow book, and Lisa felt a growing sense of unease. The room was filled with a heavy silence, interrupted only by the echo of his footsteps and the sound of rain still falling outside.

While Lisa investigated the altar, Emily checked the surroundings for any other relevant details. He found several ancient objects and esoteric decorations that seemed to be related to rituals performed in the past. Daniel took it upon himself to take notes and document everything they found.

At the base of the altar, Lisa discovered a series of hidden compartments containing various ancient objects and documents. Among the objects, there were a number of amulets and talismans, as well as a leather-bound book that appeared to be a further record of the rituals performed at the mansion.

Lisa and Emily began to go through the book and the documents found. The book contained detailed records of the esoteric ceremonies carried out by the Whitmore family, as well as instructions on how to perform the rituals and how to protect oneself from dark forces. The book also spoke of a "purification ritual" that seemed to be a crucial part of breaking the dark covenant.

Lisa was relieved to find more details about the purification ritual. The information seemed to be key to solving the mystery and protecting oneself from dark forces. The ritual required a number of specific ingredients and careful preparation, and Lisa decided that she should begin gathering the necessary elements to carry out the ritual.

As the group continued to explore the room, Lisa began to notice a number of disturbing details. The walls were covered with symbols and markings that seemed to have a connection to the dark covenant. Some of the symbols were similar to those found in the shadow book, and Lisa felt that there was a connection between the place and the events that had occurred in the mansion.

Research of the site provided a clearer view of the rituals performed by the Whitmore family and of the influence of Jonathan Blackwood. Lisa was increasingly convinced that the dark pact and esoteric rituals had had a significant impact on the history of the mansion and the mirror.

After the investigation in the room was over, the group returned to the lobby to plan the next steps. Lisa, Daniel, and Emily were exhausted but satisfied with the progress made. They knew that the purification ritual was the next crucial step in their search for answers.

As they prepared to perform the ritual, Lisa reflected on recent events and the revelations they had made. The connection between the mirror, the dark pact, and the Whitmore family's history was taking shape, but the mystery was not yet fully solved.

The fog outside had cleared, and the rain had stopped, leaving fresh and clean air. The group prepared to face the next challenge in their research, hoping that the purification ritual could offer a solution to the problems they had faced.

Lisa knew the truth was near, but she was also aware that secrets from the past could have unexpected consequences. With renewed determination and knowledge gained, Lisa was ready to face the challenges ahead and unravel the mysteries that still surrounded the mirror and the mansion.

Chapter 8

The atmosphere in the mansion had changed since the last investigation. The sense of unease that had been present for the past few days had intensified, as if the mansion itself was awaiting the outcome of the events that were unfolding. Lisa Murphy, Daniel, and Emily were in the library, preparing to perform the purification ritual described in the book of shadows.

The ritual was complex and required a number of specific ingredients, many of which Lisa and Emily had managed to gather during their research. The library was filled with jars of herbs, oils, and crystals, meticulously arranged on a table. Lisa had followed the book's instructions to the letter, making sure that each item was in the right place.

While preparing the ritual, the group discussed the details and precautions they should take. Emily, with her background in esotericism, had reviewed the ritual instructions several times and marked the key steps they needed to follow. Daniel, who had been researching the history of the mansion and the role of Jonathan Blackwood, offered his support and watched intently.

The purification ritual was designed to remove dark influences and restore balance to the mansion. It required a series of steps, starting with creating a circle of protection on the floor, around the altar Lisa had found in the basement. The circle was to be traced with a special powder that Lisa had prepared, using the protective symbols described in the book.

Lisa and Emily began to carefully trace the circle, following the instructions in the book. The atmosphere in the library was tense, and the sound of water droplets falling on the roof seemed to amplify the silence that enveloped the place. Every step of the ritual was carried out with precision, and the group was attentive to any details that could affect the success of the ritual.

Once the circle of protection was complete, Lisa placed the necessary ingredients and items on the altar. The altar was adorned with amulets, crystals, and oils that were to be used during the ritual. Emily lit a series of candles around the altar, creating an atmosphere of dim light that added a mystical touch to the process.

Lisa began to recite the words of the ritual aloud, following the text of the shadow book. The words were in an ancient language, and their pronunciation was essential for the ritual to be successful. While Lisa recited, Emily and Daniel kept watch, making sure everything was in order and that the circle of protection remained intact.

The ritual required several stages, each with its own set of instructions and actions. Lisa began with the first stage, which involved purifying the altar and objects using a mixture of oils and herbs. The mixture was applied with a special brush, and Lisa moved the brush in circular motions while reciting purification prayers.

The second stage of the ritual involved the invocation of protective energies to help counteract dark influences. Lisa used crystals and amulets to channel positive energies, placing them at specific points around the altar. Emily helped prepare a mixture of incense and herbs that needed to be burned during the process.

As the incense burned, the scent filled the library, creating an atmosphere of calm and concentration. Lisa continued to recite the words of the ritual, and the group felt a growing energy in the air. The candles flickered, and the circle of protection seemed to glow with a soft light.

In the third stage of the ritual, Lisa had to perform a series of summons to ward off the dark forces. He used a mixture of water and special essences to spray the altar and the circle of protection, following the instructions in the book. The action had to be done with precision, and Lisa was attentive to every detail.

While Lisa worked on the third stage, Emily and Daniel watched intently. The tension in the room was palpable, and the atmosphere became more intense as the ritual progressed. Lisa could sense the presence of energies in the air, and the atmosphere seemed charged with a powerful and concentrated energy.

The last stage of the ritual was to seal the protective energy and ensure that the dark covenant was neutralized. Lisa recited a series of final words as she set the amulets and crystals in place. The candlelight shone brightly, and the circle of protection seemed to radiate a vibrant energy.

With the ritual completed, the group gathered in the center of the circle of protection, exhausted but relieved. Lisa felt a sense of accomplishment at having successfully carried out the ritual, but she also knew that there were still challenges to be faced. The dark pact had been neutralized, but the mystery of the mirror and the history of the Whitmore family remained completely unsolved.

Daniel and Emily offered words of support and congratulations to Lisa, acknowledging the effort and dedication she had put into the ritual. The group was tired but satisfied with the progress made, and they prepared to continue the investigation and seek more answers.

The night was progressing and the mansion seemed to be calm after the ritual. The sound of rain had completely stopped, and the air felt fresh and clean. Lisa made her way to her room, reflecting on recent events and next steps in the investigation.

As she prepared to rest, Lisa realized that the mirror still held secrets. Although the purification ritual had been a success, the mirror remained an enigma and the connection between the dark covenant and the Whitmore family required further exploration. Lisa was determined to unravel all the mysteries and find the truth behind the mirror and the events that had marked the history of the mansion.

With renewed determination and knowledge gained, Lisa prepared to face the challenges ahead and continue her search for answers. The truth was close, but there was still much to discover and resolve in the complex web of secrets that surrounded the mansion and the mirror.

Chapter 9

The next morning was clear and bright, in contrast to the gray and rainy weather that had preceded the purification ritual. Sunlight filtered through the mansion's windows illuminated the hallways, revealing details that had remained hidden in the gloom of the night. Lisa Murphy woke up with a renewed sense of hope, knowing that the ritual had been a crucial step in solving the mystery, but there was still much to discover.

After a light breakfast, Lisa, Daniel, and Emily met in the library to continue the research. The library was full of old books and historical documents, and the group decided it was time to examine the mirror more closely. The mirror, which had been in the hall of the mansion, had been the starting point of the whole mystery, and Lisa knew that she must understand its true purpose and origin in order to solve the riddle.

Emily began to go through the notes and documents they had found in the shadow book and secret compartments. In particular, he focused on any information related to the history of the mirror and its possible connection to the esoteric rituals described in the book. Daniel, for his part, sought additional information about Jonathan Blackwood and his relationship with the mirror and the dark pact.

Lisa, meanwhile, headed to the hall to examine the mirror closely. Although the purification ritual had neutralized the dark influences, the mirror remained an enigma. Lisa wanted to understand more about her background and her role in the history of the Whitmore family.

The mirror was placed prominently in the lobby, with its ornate gilded frame and its reflective surface intact. Lisa walked over to the mirror and began to examine the details of the frame and surface. He noticed that there were inscriptions and symbols carved into the frame that seemed to have a special meaning.

With a magnifying glass in hand, Lisa studied the inscriptions on the mirror frame. The inscriptions were of an ancient language, and although Lisa could not read it directly, the images and symbols were familiar. They seemed to be related to esoteric practices and ancient rituals. Lisa wondered if these inscriptions could provide additional clues about the purpose of the mirror and its connection to the dark covenant.

While Lisa examined the mirror, Emily and Daniel continued their research in the library. Emily found a section of the shadow book that talked about the creation of esoteric mirrors and their role in rituals. The book mentioned that mirrors could be used to channel energies and reveal hidden secrets. This confirmed that the mirror had a special function in the rituals performed by the Whitmore family.

Daniel, for his part, discovered that Jonathan Blackwood had written several texts on the use of mirrors in esoteric practice. Blackwood had been an expert in manipulating energies and had used mirrors as tools to channel and control supernatural forces. The information Daniel found suggested that Blackwood had been involved in the creation of the mirror in the mansion.

With this new information, Lisa, Daniel, and Emily met to discuss their findings. The connection between the mirror, Jonathan Blackwood, and the dark pact was taking shape, but there were still many unanswered questions. Lisa shared her observations about the inscriptions on the mirror frame and the possible relationship to esoteric rituals.

Emily suggested that the next step should be to try activating the mirror to see if it could reveal more information. The shadow book had mentioned that some esoteric mirrors could be activated by specific rituals or procedures. Lisa and Emily decided they should try one of these procedures to see if they could get more answers.

The group prepared a space in the library to carry out the procedure. Lisa and Emily placed the mirror in the center of the room and prepared a series of ingredients and objects needed to activate the mirror. Daniel was in charge of documenting the process and making sure everything was in order.

The procedure began with cleaning the mirror using a special blend of oils and essences. Lisa and Emily recited a series of words in an ancient language as they applied the mixture to the mirror. The atmosphere in the library became denser, and the air seemed to vibrate with subtle energy.

Once the mirror was clean and ready, Lisa and Emily performed a series of summons to activate the mirror. They used a combination of candles, crystals, and esoteric symbols to channel the necessary energy. The mirror began to glow with a soft light, and Lisa felt a stream of energy that seemed to emanate from its surface.

As the mirror activated, Lisa and Emily watched carefully for any changes in the reflection. The surface of the mirror began to show images and patterns that appeared to be fragments of the history and events related to the mansion. The images were fuzzy and changing rapidly, but Lisa could make out a few key details.

Among the images that appeared in the mirror, Lisa saw scenes of the Whitmore family performing rituals and ceremonies in the mansion. He also saw footage of Jonathan Blackwood and his interactions with family. The images seemed to tell a story of betrayal and power, with the mirror playing a central role in the events.

Lisa, Emily, and Daniel took note of the images and tried to interpret their meaning. The information revealed by the mirror seemed to confirm that the dark pact had been made by a member of the Whitmore family in collaboration with Blackwood. The mirror had been used as a tool to channel and maintain the covenant.

With the new information gleaned from the mirror, the group felt closer to solving the mystery. However, they knew that there were still many details to be discovered. The connection between the dark covenant, the mirror, and the Whitmore family was becoming clearer, but the full truth was still out of reach.

The group decided that they should further investigate the history of Jonathan Blackwood and his relationship with the Whitmore family. It was also necessary to find more details about the dark pact and how it had affected the mansion and its inhabitants. Lisa, Daniel, and Emily were determined to continue the investigation and unravel all the secrets that still surrounded the mirror and the mansion.

The afternoon progressed and the sun began to descend, plunging the mansion in a golden light. The group prepared for the next phase of the investigation, knowing that the path to the truth was fraught with challenges and revelations. With renewed determination and information gained, Lisa was ready to face the challenges ahead and continue her search for answers.

Chapter 10

Lisa Murphy woke up with a sense of unease that she couldn't shake. The information obtained from the mirror had shed more light on the mansion's dark past, but it had also left many questions unanswered. The tale of betrayal and dark pact that I had seen in the mirror images indicated a more complex story than they had imagined. As the sun rose in the sky and the mansion began to awaken, Lisa knew they needed to delve even deeper into the story of Jonathan Blackwood and the Whitmore family.

The morning was quiet, and the group gathered in the library to discuss their next steps. Lisa, Daniel, and Emily were determined to unravel the mystery surrounding the mansion and the mirror. Daniel had found relevant information about Jonathan Blackwood in the old archives, and Emily was going through the details of the dark covenant described in the book of shadows. Lisa decided it was time to explore Blackwood's history and her relationship with the Whitmore family in greater depth.

Emily had discovered a number of documents and correspondence that appeared to be from the time Blackwood was active in the mansion. These documents included letters and notes that could provide additional information about his relationship with the Whitmore family and the purpose of the dark pact. Daniel was in charge of organizing and analyzing these documents, while Emily reviewed the correspondence for clues.

Lisa delved into the investigation of Jonathan Blackwood's story. He knew that Blackwood was a central figure in the mystery surrounding the mansion and the mirror. The information Daniel had found indicated that Blackwood had been an influential esotericist with a deep knowledge of occult practices and rituals. His relationship with the Whitmore family was key to understanding the dark pact and the role of the mirror.

Lisa found an old diary of Jonathan Blackwood's in the archives. The diary was filled with notes and reflections on his esoteric practices and his experiments with magic and rituals. As Lisa read the pages of the diary, she realized that Blackwood was obsessed with power and control, and had been looking for ways to increase his influence and power through dark rituals.

In the diary, Blackwood spoke of his association with the Whitmore family and how he had been invited to the mansion to assist in the making of a dark pact. Blackwood had promised the Whitmores that he would grant them power and fortune in exchange for their loyalty and commitment to the pact. However, as the pact progressed, the relationship between Blackwood and the family became more tense and conflicted.

Lisa also found details about the ritual that had been used to seal the dark pact. The ritual required a series of specific steps and the invocation of supernatural forces, and Blackwood had described how he had used the mirror as a tool to channel and maintain the power of the covenant. Information in the diary confirmed that the mirror was essential to the pact and that its purpose was to maintain control over the dark forces.

Emily and Daniel continued to go through correspondence and documents related to the dark covenant. They found a series of letters between Blackwood and the Whitmore family that spoke of the terms of the pact and the difficulties they had faced in the process. The letters revealed that the Whitmore family had begun to question the pact and Blackwood's influence, and there had been disagreements over how to handle the power and consequences of the pact.

The group met to discuss their findings. Lisa shared the information from Blackwood's diary and details about the dark pact and the mirror. Emily and Daniel provided a summary of the letters and documents they had found, highlighting the conflicts and tensions between Blackwood and the Whitmore family.

With the new information, the group began to make connections between past events and current problems in the mansion. The story of betrayal and power that had unfolded between Blackwood and the Whitmores seemed to be the key to solving the mystery of the mirror and the dark pact. Lisa realized that the next step in the investigation should be to examine the effects of the pact on the mansion and its inhabitants.

Lisa, Daniel, and Emily decided to further investigate the effects of the dark covenant on the mansion and how it had affected the Whitmore family. They knew that the pact had had a significant impact on the history of the mansion, and it was essential to understand how it had influenced events and the lives of the inhabitants.

The group headed to the basement of the mansion, the place where they had found the altar and esoteric symbols. Lisa and Emily wanted to examine the place in more detail to look for any additional evidence about the dark pact and its effects. Daniel took it upon himself to take notes and document any relevant findings.

While exploring the basement, Lisa and Emily found a series of markings and symbols on the walls that appeared to be related to the dark pact. The markings were similar to those found in the shadow book and in the mirror, and Lisa wondered if they could provide additional clues as to the purpose of the pact and its impact on the mansion.

In a corner of the basement, Lisa discovered a hidden compartment containing a number of old documents and objects. The documents included records and correspondence related to the dark covenant and the rituals performed by the Whitmore and Blackwood family. Among the objects, Lisa found a number of amulets and talismans that appeared to have been used in rituals.

Emily examined the documents and found a detailed record of the pact's effects on the mansion and the Whitmore family. Records indicated that the pact had had a negative impact on the health and well-being of the inhabitants of the mansion, and had caused a number of unfortunate and tragic events over the years.

The group realized that the dark pact had had devastating consequences for the Whitmore family and for the mansion. Blackwood's influence and the power of the covenant had caused a number of problems and difficulties that had affected everyone who lived in the mansion.

With this new information, Lisa, Daniel, and Emily were more determined than ever to solve the mystery and find a solution. They knew that they must undo the dark pact and free the mansion from the negative influence it had caused. The group prepared to face the next challenge in their investigation, hoping that truth and the solution to the mystery would be within reach.

Night came, and the air in the mansion grew colder. Lisa, Daniel, and Emily met in the library to plan the next steps in their research. The story of the dark pact and the impact on the mansion was taking shape, and the group was ready to continue their search for answers.

With renewed determination and knowledge gained, Lisa was ready to face the challenges ahead and unravel the secrets that still surrounded the mirror and the mansion. The truth was near, and Lisa was determined to find it, no matter what obstacles might come along the way.

Chapter 11

Night settled over the mansion, bringing with it an eerie silence that seemed to be the prelude to significant events. Lisa Murphy was in the library, surrounded by documents, books, and old artifacts, going through the information they had discovered in the basement. The light from the lamp illuminated his face with a soft glow as he studied the markings and symbols found on the walls.

Daniel and Emily had decided to take a break and explore other areas of the mansion in search of more clues. Lisa was determined to decipher the records found in the basement, hoping that they might shed more light on the dark events that had affected the Whitmore family and the dark pact with Jonathan Blackwood.

The detailed record Lisa had found included a series of notes about tragic and mysterious events that had occurred at the mansion over the years. These events appeared to be related to the influence of the dark covenant and rituals performed by Blackwood and the Whitmore family.

Among the documents, Lisa found a series of letters written by members of the Whitmore family that spoke of strange occurrences and the difficulties they had faced due to the dark pact. The letters revealed a story of despair and hopelessness, and Lisa could feel the weight of the tragedy that had befallen the family.

As she read the letters, Lisa began to notice a pattern. Tragic events and strange occurrences seemed to be concentrated on certain dates and time periods. Lisa realized that these events coincided with the dates of the rituals and ceremonies described in the book of shadows. This suggested that the dark pact had a direct impact on the events that had occurred in the mansion.

Lisa decided to review the dates and events in detail, looking for any additional connections between the rituals and the tragic events. The information revealed a series of coincidences that pointed to a dark and predictable pattern. Every time a ritual was performed or a ceremony was held, there seemed to be an increase in the intensity of the tragic events and trouble in the mansion.

As Lisa continued her research, she began to notice a change in the atmosphere of the library. The air seemed to grow heavier and denser, and a sense of unease came over her. Lisa looked around, trying to identify the source of the uneasiness, but found nothing out of the ordinary.

Suddenly, he heard a thud coming from one of the bookshelves. Lisa approached cautiously, feeling a mixture of curiosity and fear. When he reached the shelf, he saw that one of the books had fallen to the floor. He picked it up and examined it, realizing that it was an old book with a worn cover.

Lisa opened the book and found that it was full of esoteric annotations and diagrams. The notes appeared to relate to the rituals and practices described in the book of shadows. Lisa realized that the book might contain valuable information about the dark pact and how it had influenced the mansion.

The book included a series of detailed diagrams about the rituals performed by Jonathan Blackwood and the Whitmore family. The diagrams showed the different stages of the rituals and the tools used to channel the energies. Lisa began comparing the diagrams with the symbols and markings found in the basement, looking for matches.

As Lisa reviewed the book, she noticed that there were a series of diagrams and notes that spoke of a final ritual that needed to be performed to seal the dark pact permanently. The final ritual was designed to neutralize the influence of the pact and free the mansion from the dark forces that had been summoned.

Lisa realized that the final ritual was a crucial part of solving the mystery. If he could carry out the final ritual successfully, they would be able to undo the dark pact and put an end to the negative influence on the mansion. With this new information, Lisa felt more hopeful and determined to find a solution.

While Lisa was engrossed in her reading, Daniel and Emily returned to the library. They had been exploring other areas of the mansion and had found some additional documents and ancient objects. Daniel had discovered a series of letters from the Whitmore family that spoke of a last-ditch attempt to undo the dark covenant. The cards mentioned performing a final ritual and searching for an ancient artifact that could be the key to completing the ritual.

Emily had also found an old logbook that contained information about the tragic and mysterious events that had occurred at the mansion. The records confirmed the dates and patterns Lisa had identified in documents found in the basement.

The group met to share their findings and discuss next steps. Lisa explained the importance of the final ritual and how it could be the key to solving the mystery of the dark pact. Daniel and Emily shared the information about the cards and the aforementioned artifact, which seemed to be essential to completing the ritual.

The artifact mentioned in the letters appeared to be an ancient relic that had been used in the Whitmore family's rituals. The group decided that they should search for the artifact and make sure it was available for the final ritual. They knew that the artifact might be hidden somewhere in the mansion or in the surrounding area.

With the new information and renewed determination, the group began planning their search for the artifact and preparing for the final ritual. The night continued, and the mansion seemed to be calm, as if waiting for the resolution of the mysteries that surrounded it.

Lisa, Daniel, and Emily prepared to face the upcoming challenges in their investigation, hoping that the truth and the solution to the mystery would be within reach. The search for the artifact and the performance of the final ritual were the crucial next steps in his mission to undo the dark pact and free the mansion from its negative influence.

The night was full of promises and secrets, and the group was determined to unravel them. With each revelation and discovery, Lisa grew closer to solving the enigma of the mirror and the mansion's dark past. The truth was near, and Lisa was ready to face whatever came her way, no matter how challenging the path to resolution might be.

Chapter 12

The next morning he woke up with clear skies and bright sunshine that promised a day of clarity and purpose. Lisa Murphy, Daniel, and Emily woke up with the feeling that time was of the essence. They knew they had to act quickly to find the ancient artifact needed for the final ritual, and with it, solve the mystery that shrouded the mansion and the dark pact.

After a frugal breakfast, the group met in the library to review the information obtained and plan their search. Lisa had exhaustively reviewed the documents and books they had found, and had come up with a plan to explore the mansion in search of the artifact. The artifact, according to letters found by Daniel, could be hidden in a place significant to the Whitmore family or related to esoteric rituals.

The first step was to review the documents and notes Daniel had found, which mentioned a last attempt to undo the dark pact and the search for the artifact. These documents indicated that the artifact was related to an ancient ritual and that its location could be connected to the tragic events that occurred in the mansion.

The group decided to begin their search in the oldest and least explored areas of the mansion. The mansion, with its intricate network of hallways, basements, and hidden rooms, offered plenty of places where the artifact might be hidden. They knew that every corner of the mansion could be crucial to solving the mystery.

Lisa, Daniel, and Emily started in the basement, the place where they had found the esoteric documents and symbols. They checked the corners of the basement again, looking for any additional clues that might have been overlooked. Despite their efforts, they found nothing that appeared to be directly related to the artifact.

Discouraged but not defeated, the group decided to move to the upper floor of the mansion. There, Lisa and Emily began exploring a series of old rooms and closets. The rooms were filled with old furniture, decorative objects, and memorabilia from times past, but the group found no relevant clues.

Meanwhile, Daniel went through the old records and letters they had found. There was a pattern to the dates and events that mentioned certain rooms and areas of the mansion. Daniel noticed that one of the letters spoke of a specific event that had occurred in one of the rooms upstairs. This room had been mentioned as a significant place during the performance of one of the important rituals.

With this new information, the group went to the room mentioned in the documents. The room was located in a corner away from the mansion and seemed to have been little used in recent years. Upon entering, Lisa, Daniel, and Emily found a series of antique furniture covered in dust and cobwebs.

Lisa went to an old closet in the corner of the room and began to examine it. The closet was filled with old clothes and objects that appeared to be family mementos. Lisa carefully checked each shelf, and suddenly found a wooden box at the top of the cabinet. The box was covered in dust and seemed to have been hidden for a long time.

Lisa took the box carefully and brought it to the table in the center of the room. Emily and Daniel looked at her expectantly as Lisa opened the box. Inside the box, they found a number of ancient objects, including an amulet, a candle, and a number of documents that appeared to be related to esoteric rituals.

One of the documents was an old map of the mansion with a series of markings and symbols indicating important locations. The map seemed to show a secret passageway that connected different areas of the mansion. Lisa and Daniel studied the map carefully, looking for any clues as to where the artifact might be hidden.

The group decided to follow the map and explore the indicated secret passageway. With the help of the flashlight, they began to search for the entrance to the passageway, which seemed to be hidden behind a false wall in one of the nearby rooms. After a thorough search, they found a lever hidden in a corner of the wall that, when activated, revealed a secret door.

Lisa, Daniel, and Emily walked through the door and into the dark, narrow passageway. The passageway was full of cobwebs and dust, and it seemed to have been dormant for a long time. As they advanced, the group kept their senses alert for any signs of the artifact.

The passageway led to a small underground chamber that was decorated with esoteric symbols and ancient markings. In the center of the chamber was a pedestal on which rested an ancient wooden chest. The chest was adorned with intricate engravings and appeared to be the kind of object they could have used in rituals.

Lisa, Daniel, and Emily approached the chest cautiously. Lisa took the key she had found in the wooden box in the previous room and used it to open the chest. Inside the chest, they found an object that appeared to be the artifact mentioned in the documents: an ancient relic that was surrounded by esoteric symbols and ornaments.

The artifact was a crystal sphere with an intricate metal frame, and its surface was engraved with ancient symbols and runes. The group examined it closely, recognizing that this item was crucial to the final ritual they were to perform to undo the dark pact.

With the artifact in hand, the group decided to return to the library to prepare the final ritual. They knew that the ritual would be complex and require careful planning to make sure everything was carried out correctly. Lisa, Daniel, and Emily were determined to complete the task and solve the mystery of the mansion.

As they returned to the library, Lisa reflected on the events that had led to this point. The search for the artifact had been challenging, but the discovery of the key object brought them closer to solving the enigma. With the artifact in their possession, the group felt more hopeful and prepared to face the next challenge.

The day was coming to an end, and the mansion seemed to be calm, as if waiting for the outcome of the events that had unfolded. Lisa, Daniel, and Emily prepared for the final ritual, aware that time was pressing and that the truth was at hand.

The search for the artifact had been successful, and now the group was ready to face the final ritual and undo the dark pact that had plagued the mansion for so long. With determination and hope, Lisa prepared for the next step in her mission, knowing that solving the mystery was closer than ever.

Chapter 13

Twilight spread over the mansion, covering its ancient walls with a soft, elongated shadow. The atmosphere in the mansion was dense with anticipation of the upcoming ritual. Lisa Murphy, Daniel, and Emily were in the library, surrounded by documents, books, and the ancient artifact they had found in the secret passageway. The air was filled with a mixture of nervousness and hope, as the group prepared to perform the final ritual that could undo the dark pact and free the mansion from its negative influence.

Lisa was sitting at the library table, reviewing the instructions for the final ritual she had found in the documents and the ancient book. The information was complex and detailed, and the ritual required a series of specific steps and the use of the artifact to channel the energies needed to break the dark pact. Lisa was focused on making sure she understood every detail of the ritual, knowing that any mistake could have disastrous consequences.

Daniel and Emily were busy preparing the space for the ritual. They had cleared an area in the center of the library and were placing the necessary objects according to the instructions of the ritual. There were candles, esoteric symbols, and several additional components that had to be used to perform the ritual successfully.

The artifact, the glass sphere with the intricate metal frame, rested in the center of the table, surrounded by the necessary components. Lisa looked at him with a mixture of wonder and respect, recognizing his importance in the performance of the ritual. The artifact seemed to emit a dim light, which created a subtle glow in the room.

While the group worked, Emily reviewed documents and notes to make sure everything was in order. Daniel was in charge of placing the candles and esoteric symbols on the ground, following the precise instructions of the ritual. The atmosphere in the library became more and more solemn, as the group prepared to face the challenge ahead.

The final ritual required a series of specific steps, including the invocation of supernatural forces and the use of the artifact to channel and dispel dark energies. Lisa went through each step carefully, making sure everyone understood their role in the ritual and was prepared to carry out each task with precision.

As the sun set and night fell on the mansion, the group gathered to discuss the final details of the ritual. Lisa explained each stage of the process and stressed the importance of staying focused and following instructions accurately. They knew that the success of the ritual depended on their ability to work in harmony and execute each step correctly.

With the space prepared and the artifact in place, the group was ready to begin the ritual. Lisa lit the candles and placed the esoteric symbols on the ground, following the pattern indicated in the documents. Emily and Daniel stood in designated positions around the ritual area, ready to begin when Lisa gave the signal.

Lisa took a deep breath and began to recite the words of the ritual, following the instructions of the ancient book. The atmosphere in the library seemed to vibrate with increasing energy, as the candles emitted a dim light that illuminated the esoteric symbols on the ground. The crystal sphere in the center of the table began to glow with increasing intensity, casting dancing shadows on the walls.

The group remained focused as Lisa continued to recite the words of the ritual. The candles flickered and the atmosphere became more and more charged with palpable energy. As the ritual progressed, Lisa began to feel a connection to the supernatural forces that were being invoked. The crystal sphere seemed to resonate with a deep and powerful vibration, and Lisa could feel how the artifact was channeling the energy needed to undo the dark pact.

Suddenly, a change in the atmosphere became apparent. The shadows on the walls seemed to move and twist, as if responding to the energy of the ritual. The air became colder and the feeling of discomfort intensified. Lisa and the group continued with the ritual, undeterred by the disturbances.

The critical moment of the ritual came when Lisa had to use the artifact to channel the energy and break the dark pact. Lisa took the crystal sphere and lifted it above her head, following the instructions in the ancient book. The sphere shone with an intense light, and the energy in the library reached its peak.

Lisa recited the last words of the ritual with determination, as the crystal sphere emitted a burst of light and energy. The shadows on the walls seemed to dissipate and the air became lighter. The group felt a growing relief as the ritual moved toward its conclusion.

Finally, the ritual came to an end and the crystal sphere stopped shining. The candles went out, and the energy in the library began to calm down. The group looked at each other with a mixture of exhaustion and relief, knowing that they had completed the final ritual.

Lisa, Daniel, and Emily took a moment to catch their breath and process what had just happened. The ritual had been a challenge, but the group was satisfied to have carried it out successfully. They knew that the dark covenant's influence had been dispelled and that the mansion was free from the negative influence that had plagued the Whitmore family for so long.

With the ritual complete, the group decided to take some time to rest and reflect on the events that had led to this point. The mansion seemed to be calm, and the air felt lighter and fresher. Lisa, Daniel, and Emily were grateful to have overcome the challenge and were ready to face the next steps in their mission.

The night progressed and the mansion began to regain its tranquility. Lisa looked around the library, feeling a deep sense of accomplishment and peace. He knew that the mystery of the mirror and the dark pact had been solved, and that the mansion was finally free from the influence of the dark forces.

The group prepared to rest and recover, knowing that they had accomplished a significant feat. With the ritual complete and the truth revealed, Lisa, Daniel, and Emily were ready to face any challenges that might arise and move on with their lives, knowing that they had made a major difference in the mansion's history.

Chapter 14

The next morning dawned calm and clear. Sunlight filtered through the mansion's windows, bathing the rooms in a warm, comforting glow. Lisa Murphy, Daniel, and Emily woke up feeling refreshed after the previous night's grueling ritual. The success of the final ritual had brought an air of relief to the mansion, and the sense of heaviness that had been present for so long seemed to have dissipated.

After a light breakfast, the group met in the library to discuss next steps. They had completed the ritual, but they knew that there were still unanswered questions and aspects of the mystery that needed to be cleared up. The mansion had been freed from the influence of the dark pact, but the past remained an enigma that needed to be solved.

Lisa, with a look of determination on her face, began to review again the documents and letters they had found throughout their research. I knew there were important details that could shed more light on the history of the Whitmore family and Jonathan Blackwood's role in the dark pact. As she examined the documents, Lisa realized that she had overlooked some letters and notes that might contain valuable information.

Daniel and Emily were also going through the documents, looking for additional clues about the history of the mansion and the Whitmore family. Emily, in particular, was interested in letters and records that mentioned key events and people in the mansion's history. Daniel, on the other hand, was focused on the esoteric notes and symbols they had found, trying to better understand how they had influenced the rituals.

Lisa found a letter that had been written by a member of the Whitmore family in the 19th century. The letter mentioned a significant event that had occurred in the mansion that was related to the dark pact. The letter spoke of a secret meeting that had taken place at the mansion, where important matters about the covenant and its impact on the family had been discussed.

The letter also mentioned an old diary that had been hidden in the mansion by one of the family members. The diary contained details about the events that had led to the dark pact and the decisions that had been made by members of the Whitmore family. Lisa realized that the diary might contain crucial information about the family's history and the dark pact.

With the new clue in hand, Lisa, Daniel, and Emily decided to look for the diary mentioned in the letter. The search led them to explore additional areas of the mansion, including rooms and spaces that had not yet been thoroughly reviewed. The mansion, with its many hidden nooks and crannies, offered many places where the diary might be hidden.

The search began in the attic, an area that had been used as storage over the years. The attic was full of boxes, antique furniture and forgotten objects. Lisa, Daniel, and Emily began to go through the boxes and shelves for anything that might contain the journal.

After several hours of searching, they found an antique box at the back of the loft. The box was covered in dust and cobwebs, and it seemed to have been in the attic for a long time. Lisa opened the box carefully, and inside she found a number of old documents and objects, including a time-worn diary.

The diary was bound in leather and appeared to have been handwritten. Lisa examined it carefully and began to read the entries, which were written in elegant and detailed calligraphy. The diary contained accounts of the events that had led to the dark pact and the Whitmore family's infighting.

As Lisa read the diary entries, she discovered startling details about the family's history. The diary revealed that the dark pact had initially been made in a desperate attempt to save the family from a series of tragedies and misfortunes. However, as the pact progressed, its effects became increasingly damaging and devastating.

The diary also mentioned the existence of a second crystal sphere, which had been used in the initial rituals of the pact. This sphere was designed to balance the energies and prevent the covenant from becoming too powerful. However, the sphere had been lost or hidden somewhere in the mansion, and its whereabouts had been forgotten over time.

Lisa, Daniel, and Emily realized that the second crystal sphere could be crucial to fully understanding the history of the covenant and the Whitmore family. With this new information, they decided to continue their search in the mansion, hoping to find the second sphere and solve the riddle completely.

The group headed to other areas of the mansion that had not yet been thoroughly explored. Lisa went through the documents and diary notes, looking for clues to the whereabouts of the second sphere. Daniel and Emily concentrated on sifting through the hidden passageways and rooms, looking for any signs of the missing sphere.

During the search, they found a number of rooms and spaces that had been sealed or blocked off for many years. Some of these areas contained antique artifacts and memorabilia from the Whitmore family, while others were empty and cluttered. The search was meticulous and thorough, but the group was determined to find the missing sphere.

Finally, after several hours of searching, Lisa discovered a secret room in the basement of the mansion. The room was hidden behind a false wall and contained a number of ancient objects and artifacts related to the rituals and the dark pact. In the center of the room was a pedestal on which rested a crystal sphere matching the description in the diary.

Lisa, Daniel, and Emily examined the sphere carefully, recognizing that it was the second sphere mentioned in the diary. The sphere was adorned with esoteric symbols and seemed to be designed to balance energies. The group was relieved and excited to find the lost object.

With the second sphere in their possession, the group returned to the library to analyze the information and documents found. Lisa went through the diary and notes, trying to understand how the second sphere fit into the history of the dark covenant and the Whitmore family.

The group decided that the next stage of their research would be to carry out a detailed analysis of the sphere and its properties. They knew that the sphere could offer additional information about the covenant and the history of the mansion. With the diary, spheres, and documents in hand, Lisa, Daniel, and Emily were ready to continue their mission and solve the mystery completely.

The mansion, now freed from the influence of the dark covenant, seemed to offer new opportunities to uncover the truth. With each revelation and discovery, the group grew closer to understanding the full history of the Whitmore family and the impact of the dark covenant on their lives.

Chapter 15

The discovery of the second crystal sphere had brought a new air of hope and resolve to the group. The next morning, Lisa, Daniel, and Emily sat in the library to further examine the sphere found in the basement. They knew that this sphere could hold additional clues to unravel the secrets of the dark pact and the true legacy of the Whitmore family.

The library, which had been the center of his research, was filled with documents and artifacts that were intertwined with the history of the mansion. The sun's rays streamed through the windows, illuminating shelves full of old books and esoteric objects they had found. The atmosphere was one of concentration and determination, as the group prepared to unravel the enigma of the family's legacy.

Lisa examined the second crystal sphere carefully, noticing that it was adorned with symbols similar to those on the sphere they had used in the final ritual. The dial had a series of engravings that appeared to represent a map or a series of directions. It was evident that this sphere had a specific purpose and a crucial connection to the history of the dark covenant.

Daniel was engrossed in reviewing documents related to the dial, looking for clues that might help to understand its function. Emily, for her part, would go through the diary notes they had found, trying to find any details that might shed light on the meaning of the symbols on the dial.

After thorough analysis, the group discovered that the symbols on the sphere represented different locations within the mansion and its surroundings. Some of the symbols matched places they had already explored, while others seemed to point to areas they hadn't yet investigated in detail.

Lisa and Emily decided to follow the clues provided by the sphere and journal to explore the locations indicated by the symbols. They knew that each location could contain crucial information about the Whitmore family's legacy and the dark pact. Daniel stayed in the library to continue analyzing the documents and prepare for any further findings.

The first location indicated by the sphere was a small chapel located in a secluded section of the mansion's garden. The chapel, which had been used as a place of worship and meditation by the Whitmore family, appeared to have been in disuse for many years. Lisa and Emily made their way to the garden, traversing paths covered with leaves and shrubs that seemed to have been neglected.

Upon arriving at the chapel, Lisa and Emily found the front door locked, but discovered a small broken window through which they were able to enter. The chapel was in a state of neglect, with dust-covered benches and cobwebs hanging from the ceiling. In the center of the chapel was an altar, and above it were a number of ancient objects and esoteric symbols.

Lisa and Emily began to check the objects on the altar and the symbols on the walls of the chapel. They found a series of engravings and drawings that seemed to be related to the rituals that had taken place in the mansion. They also found a series of documents and parchments that were wrapped in an ancient cloth.

Upon unrolling the scrolls, Lisa and Emily discovered that they contained detailed instructions on esoteric rituals and practices performed by the Whitmore family. These documents offered a deeper insight into how the rituals had been carried out and how the dark covenant had developed over time.

Among the documents, Lisa found a handwritten note that appeared to be a letter from one of the Whitmore family members. The letter spoke of an attempt to break the dark covenant and restore balance in the family. The family member had left instructions for the use of a third crystal sphere, which had been lost or hidden somewhere in the mansion.

With this new information, Lisa and Emily realized that the Whitmore family's legacy was even more intricate than they had imagined. The third crystal sphere could be key to fully understanding the dark pact and the events that had occurred in the mansion.

The group decided to return to the library and continue researching with the newly discovered information. Lisa, Daniel, and Emily were determined to find the third sphere and solve the riddle of the Whitmore family's legacy. They knew that each discovery brought them closer to understanding the truth behind the dark pact and the history of the mansion.

The next location indicated by the sphere was an ancient ceremonial hall located in a secluded corner of the mansion. The room, which had been used for important events and family rituals, was now in disuse and covered in dust. The group headed to the room to investigate and look for any clues that might be related to the third sphere.

Upon entering the ceremony room, Lisa, Daniel, and Emily found a number of antique objects and furniture that had been used at important events. The room was filled with memories of times gone by, and the group began to scan every corner for the third sphere.

After a thorough search, they found a secret compartment on the floor of the living room. The compartment was covered by an antique carpet and contained a wooden box with a padlock. Lisa used one of the keys they had previously found to open the box, and inside they found the third crystal sphere.

The third sphere was similar to the other two, but had a unique design and was adorned with additional symbols representing a number of important events and places in the history of the Whitmore family. The group was thrilled to find the sphere and decided to take it back to the library to examine it in more detail.

With all three spheres in their possession, Lisa, Daniel, and Emily knew they were close to solving the riddle of the Whitmore family's legacy and the dark pact. The spheres could provide a more complete view of how the rituals had been carried out and how the covenant could be broken definitively.

The group continued their research in the library, reviewing the documents and symbols on the spheres. Each sphere seemed to have a specific purpose and a connection to the events and rituals that had occurred in the mansion. With each discovery, the group grew closer to understanding the truth behind the dark pact and the legacy of the Whitmore family.

The mansion, now free from the influence of the dark pact, offered new opportunities to discover the truth. Lisa, Daniel, and Emily were determined to continue their mission and solve the mystery completely. With the three spheres and the information obtained, they were ready to face the final challenge and unravel the enigma of the Whitmore family's legacy.

Chapter 16

The library, illuminated by the morning light, had been transformed into a center of frenetic research. Lisa, Daniel, and Emily had gathered all the documents, crystal spheres, and notes related to the history of the dark covenant and the Whitmore family. The atmosphere was charged with anticipation as the group prepared to unravel the enigma that had been shrouded in mystery for so long.

The three crystal spheres rested on a table in the center of the library, each adorned with esoteric symbols and intricate patterns. Lisa, Daniel, and Emily sat around the table, going through the documents and comparing the symbols on the spheres with the details found on the scrolls and the journal.

The first sphere, which they had used in the final ritual, had displayed a series of symbols representing different energies and directions. The second sphere, discovered in the chapel, contained symbols related to esoteric rituals and practices. The third sphere, found in the ceremonial hall, had a unique design that depicted important events in the history of the Whitmore family.

Lisa began analyzing the symbols on the spheres, looking for patterns that could connect the events and places mentioned in the documents. Daniel would go through the diary notes, trying to identify any references to the symbols and how they had been used in rituals. Emily examined the esoteric objects and symbols found in the chapel and ceremony hall, looking for additional connections.

After several hours of research, Lisa noticed a pattern in the symbols on the spheres. Each sphere seemed to be related to a specific aspect of the dark covenant and the history of the Whitmore family. The first sphere represented the balance of energies, the second sphere was related to rituals, and the third sphere seemed to be connected to key events and decisions.

With this information, Lisa decided it was time to try a new ritual using the three spheres. They knew that the dark pact had been an attempt to balance energies and save the Whitmore family, but it had also caused great suffering and tragedy. The new ritual could be the key to solving the riddle and bringing ultimate peace to the mansion.

The group prepared the space in the library for the ritual. They placed the spheres in the center of the table, surrounded by candles and esoteric symbols. Lisa reviewed the instructions for the ritual, making sure everything was in order. Daniel and Emily were in charge of placing the objects and preparing the space according to the indications of the ritual.

When everything was ready, Lisa began to recite the words of the ritual, following the instructions in the diary and the documents found. The spheres began to glow with a dim light, and the energy in the library became palpable. Lisa and the group remained focused as they carried out each step of the ritual.

The ritual required channeling the energies of the three spheres to balance the forces and undo the dark pact. Lisa recited the words precisely, as the spheres emitted an intense light that filled the room. The group felt a growing connection to the energies and historical events that were unraveling.

As the ritual progressed, the shadows in the library began to move and twist, as if responding to the energy of the ritual. The light from the spheres became brighter, projecting complex patterns onto the walls and floor. The atmosphere was filled with a sense of power and liberation.

Lisa, Daniel, and Emily continued with the ritual, each in their designated role. The sphere that represented the balance of energies was in the center, while the other two spheres were placed in strategic positions to channel the energies. The group recited the words of the ritual and performed the necessary movements to complete each step.

Finally, the critical moment of the ritual came when Lisa had to use the spheres to balance the energies and break the dark pact definitively. He took the spheres in his hands and raised them above his head, following the instructions of the ritual. The spheres glowed with overwhelming intensity, and the energy in the library reached its peak.

Lisa recited the last words of the ritual with determination, as the spheres emitted a burst of light and energy. The shadows on the walls dissipated and the air became lighter. The group felt a wave of relief and peace as the ritual came to a close.

With the ritual complete, the spheres stopped glowing and the energy in the library calmed down. Lisa, Daniel, and Emily looked at each other with a mixture of exhaustion and satisfaction, knowing that they had successfully completed the ritual and undone the dark pact. The mansion seemed to be calm, and the negative influence had completely disappeared.

The group decided to take a moment to reflect on the events that had led to this point. They knew that the riddle of the Whitmore family's legacy had been solved and that the truth had been revealed. The mansion was free from the influence of the dark covenant and the Whitmore family's legacy had been restored.

With the success of the ritual and the truth discovered, Lisa, Daniel, and Emily were ready to face the future and move on with their lives. The mansion, now peaceful, offered new opportunities to discover and explore. The group was grateful to have overcome the challenge and was prepared for any new challenges that might arise.

The sun was setting over the mansion, bathing the rooms in a golden glow. Lisa, Daniel, and Emily were relieved and hopeful, knowing that they had made a significant difference in the history of the Whitmore family and the mansion. With the legacy puzzle solved and the dark pact undone, they were ready to begin a new chapter in their lives.

Chapter 17

After the successful ritual, the atmosphere in the mansion had changed. The darkness that had enveloped the place for so long had dissipated, giving way to a sense of calm and serenity. Lisa, Daniel, and Emily were in the library, reviewing the latest details of the Whitmore family's legacy and reflecting on recent events. Despite the sense of relief, an echo of unease lingered, as if the last fragments of the past still needed to be faced.

Lisa was going through the documents they had found in the chapel and ceremony room, trying to gather as much information as possible to fully understand the impact of the dark covenant on the Whitmore family. Daniel stood at the table, analyzing the notes and esoteric symbols carefully, while Emily examined the ancient objects that had been recovered during the investigation.

Suddenly, the library door opened, and Dr. William Whitmore, the last known descendant of the family, walked in with a grave expression. He had been absent for much of the investigation, but had been contacted by Lisa and the group as the end of the ritual approached. Dr. Whitmore, with his graceful bearing and tired look, seemed to have borne a considerable weight throughout this process.

"How did it all go?" asked Dr. Whitmore, his voice echoing in the empty space of the library.

Lisa got up and walked over to Dr. Whitmore. "We have completed the ritual and we have found all the spheres. The dark covenant's influence has worn off, but we still need to work out some details about his family's legacy."

Dr. Whitmore nodded slowly and walked toward the table where Lisa and Daniel were working. "I am willing to help in any way I can. There are aspects of the past that I need to understand, and it seems that you have reached the bottom of the mystery."

With the arrival of Dr. Whitmore, the group decided to go through the ancient documents and objects together, hoping to shed light on the last pieces of the puzzle. Dr. Whitmore sat down with them and began to examine the scrolls and letters, their knowledge of family history providing valuable perspective.

While they were going through the documents, Daniel discovered a letter hidden among the papers, a letter they hadn't noticed before. The letter was written in a personal tone and appeared to have been addressed to a member of the Whitmore family. Upon reading it, the group discovered that it contained a confession from a former family member about his role in the dark pact.

The letter revealed that the pact had initially been made in an attempt to save the family from a series of tragedies, but it also contained an element of greed and ambition. The family member had admitted to seeking power and control through the pact, which had led to the devastating consequences that had plagued the Whitmore family over the years.

Dr. Whitmore looked disturbed by the revelation, his face pale as he read the letter. "I never imagined that my family's history would be so tinged with greed and despair," he said in a trembling voice. "I always knew there was something dark in the past, but this letter confirms my worst fears."

Lisa placed a hand on Dr. Whitmore's shoulder in support. "It's important to face the truth, no matter how painful it is. Now that we know the truth, we can work to heal and restore what has been lost."

The group continued to review the documents, finding more details about the events that had led to the dark pact and how it had affected the Whitmore family. Each discovery seemed to shed light on earlier aspects of the covenant and the decisions that had been made by family members.

Among the documents, they found an ancient ritual book that contained instructions for performing the rituals used in the dark covenant. The book was filled with symbols and annotations, and appeared to be a comprehensive guide to the esoteric practices that had been used to keep the covenant.

Emily began to examine the book carefully, looking for any additional information that might be relevant. As he turned the pages, he discovered a chapter that seemed to be related to the breaking of the covenant and the restoration of balance. The information in the chapter was detailed and provided a different approach to undoing the covenant, suggesting that there was an alternative method that had not been used during the final ritual.

The group decided to investigate the alternative method described in the ritual book. Although they had already completed the final ritual, they knew that it was important to understand all aspects of the dark pact to ensure that no loose ends were left behind. The alternative method could offer additional insight into how balance could be more fully restored.

Lisa, Daniel, and Emily prepared to carry out the new approach to the ritual. Although they weren't sure if it would be necessary, they were determined to do everything they could to ensure that the dark pact had been completely undone. They prepared the space in the library, gathering the necessary objects and symbols according to the instructions in the ritual book.

Dr. Whitmore watched the process with interest and concern, aware of the importance of what they were about to do. Although the mansion already seemed to be calm, the group knew it was critical to ensure that all aspects of the dark pact had been addressed.

The new ritual began with the recitation of words and the placement of objects in specific positions. The crystal spheres were used to channel the energies, and the group carefully followed the instructions in the ritual book. Although the ritual seemed similar to the one they had previously performed, the alternative method required a series of additional steps and a different approach.

As the ritual progressed, the energy in the library began to change. The group felt a greater intensity in the spheres and a deeper connection to the historical events that were being addressed. The atmosphere was charged with power and resonated with a sense of restoration.

Finally, the ritual came to its conclusion, and the spheres ceased to shine. The energy in the library calmed down, and the group felt a sense of peace and resolution. Lisa, Daniel, and Emily looked at each other, knowing that they had addressed all aspects of the dark pact and the legacy of the Whitmore family.

Dr. Whitmore approached the group with an expression of gratitude and relief. "Thank you for everything you have done. The truth has been revealed, and my family's legacy has been restored. I am indebted to you for your dedication and effort."

Lisa smiled and nodded. "We have done the best we can to solve the mystery and bring peace to the mansion. Now is the time to move on and face the future."

With the enigma of the legacy solved and the dark pact undone, Lisa, Daniel, and Emily knew they had completed an important mission. The mansion was calm, and the past had been confronted definitively. The group prepared to close this chapter and move on to new beginnings.

Chapter 18

The sun had set over Whitmore Manor, bathing the landscape in a soft golden light that seemed to mark the end of an era of darkness and mystery. The mansion, now calm after the final ritual, offered an air of serenity that contrasted sharply with the tension and chaos that had dominated the previous days. Lisa, Daniel, and Emily, having completed much of their mission, were preparing for the final stage of their investigation: a final test that could reveal the true impact of the dark pact on the Whitmore family.

During the previous days, they had reviewed all the documents and symbols related to the dark pact and the family's legacy. They had found additional clues that suggested there might still be aspects of the covenant that needed to be confronted or understood. Although the negative energy had disappeared and the ritual had been completed, there was a lingering feeling that something was still not completely resolved.

Dr. Whitmore, aware of the importance of dealing with the past thoroughly, had decided to participate in this last test. He knew that the secrets hidden in the mansion could have significant repercussions, and he was willing to do everything he could to ensure that his family's legacy was fully restored.

The final test was to explore an area of the mansion that had been previously sealed off and whose entrance had been blocked for years. It was an ancient underground hall, mentioned in some of the ancient documents as a crucial place for the history of the dark covenant. Although the group had already explored many areas of the mansion, this underground hall was still an enigma.

Lisa, Daniel, Emily, and Dr. Whitmore made their way to the entrance of the underground hall, located in the basement of the mansion. The door was sealed with a series of ancient mechanisms that required a combination of symbols and words to be unlocked. They used clues gleaned from documents and crystal spheres to decipher the correct combination.

Once the door opened, the group descended a staircase that led to a large, dark underground hall. The air in the hall was charged with a dense energy, and the atmosphere seemed heavy with the history that had been trapped in that place.

Upon entering the living room, the group found a series of shelves and display cases filled with old objects and documents. The decoration of the place was elaborate and detailed, with esoteric symbols carved into the walls and floor. In the center of the hall was an antique altar, covered with a dark velvet cloth.

Lisa walked over to the altar and began to examine the objects above it. He found a number of esoteric artifacts and documents that seemed to be related to rituals and practices that had been carried out in the past. Among the items, there was an ancient box with a padlock that seemed to be the key to understanding the last stage of the dark pact.

Carefully, Lisa and Dr. Whitmore attempted to open the box using a combination of symbols and words. After several attempts, they managed to unlock the lock and open the box. Inside, they found an antique book with a worn leather cover and a set of handwritten letters.

The book was full of details about the esoteric rituals and practices used by the Whitmore family. It contained instructions for carrying out specific ceremonies and maintaining the balance of energies. The handwritten letters were correspondences between family members and contained information about the evolution of the dark pact over the years.

Lisa began to read the letters, discovering additional details about the sacrifices and decisions that had been made to keep the covenant. The correspondence revealed that the covenant had evolved and changed over time, and that family members had attempted to keep it under control through secret rituals and practices.

Among the letters, Lisa found one that was particularly relevant. It was a letter written by a member of the Whitmore family who had been involved in the creation of the original covenant. The letter contained a confession about the true purpose of the covenant and the way it had been used to manipulate and control family members.

Dr. Whitmore, upon reading the letter, realized that the covenant had originally been created with the intent of protecting the family, but had become corrupted over time. The family member had admitted that he had used the pact to gain power and control, which had led to the tragedies that had plagued the Whitmore family for generations.

Lisa, Daniel, and Emily realized that the ultimate test was to confront the legacy of the covenant and make decisions about how to restore balance completely. They knew that the truth about the covenant had to be revealed and accepted, and that it was critical to face any final issues that might have been left unresolved.

The group decided to hold a final ceremony in the underground hall, using the objects and documents found to carry out a restoration ritual. The ritual aimed to release any residual energy related to the dark pact and close the chapter of the story definitively.

With Dr. Whitmore acting as a witness and participant in the ceremony, Lisa, Daniel, and Emily began preparing the space for the ritual. They placed the esoteric objects on the altar and recited the words of the ritual carefully, following the instructions of the ancient book and handwritten letters.

As the ritual progressed, the energy in the underground hall began to change. The shadows on the walls seemed to move and twist, as if responding to the energy of the ritual. The group felt a growing connection to the historical events and decisions that had led to the dark pact.

Finally, the ritual came to a conclusion, and the group felt a sense of liberation and peace. The residual energies related to the dark covenant had dissipated, and the Whitmore family's legacy had been fully restored. The underground hall, once filled with darkness and mystery, had been transformed into a place of calm and resolution.

Dr. Whitmore approached the group with an expression of gratitude and relief. "Thank you for everything you have done. The truth has been revealed and my family's legacy has been restored. I am indebted to you for your dedication and effort."

Lisa smiled and nodded. "We have faced the past and restored balance. Now is the time to move forward and build a new future."

With the last test completed and the Whitmore family legacy restored, Lisa, Daniel, and Emily prepared to close this chapter of their investigation. The mansion, now peaceful, offered new opportunities to discover and explore. The group was grateful to have risen to the challenge and was ready to face the future with hope and determination.

Chapter 19

The next morning was bright and clear, with the sun shining on Whitmore Manor and its environs. The group, though exhausted from the intense days of research and rituals, was filled with a new sense of relief and hope. They had managed to confront and undo the dark pact that had plagued the Whitmore family for generations, and the family's legacy had been restored. Now, the challenge was to face a future full of possibilities and rebuild their lives after this experience.

Lisa, Daniel, Emily, and Dr. Whitmore were in the main hall of the mansion, which had been restored to its former glory. The atmosphere was filled with a fresh air, and the group felt relieved and hopeful as they discussed the next steps to take.

Lisa, with a satisfied expression on her face, looked around the room. "It seems incredible how the mansion has changed. The air is much lighter and the atmosphere feels completely different."

Daniel nodded, looking at the place with interest. "Yes, the restoration has been a success. But now it's time to think about how to move forward and use what we've learned."

Emily, who had been going through some of the documents found in the mansion, approached the group with a proposal. "I've been thinking about the possibility of documenting everything we've discovered. The story of the Whitmore family and the dark pact is fascinating and worth sharing."

Dr. Whitmore, who had been silent for much of the conversation, chimed in with a thoughtful look. "That could be an excellent idea. The truth must be known and understood so that the past does not repeat itself. In addition, documenting history could help educate others about the dangers of dark pacts and esoteric practices."

Lisa agreed with the proposal. "Documenting everything we have learned could serve as a warning and a guide for future generations. It could also help heal and restore the image of the Whitmore family."

The group decided to work together to collect all relevant information and documents, creating a comprehensive archive on the dark pact and its impact on the Whitmore family. Dr. Whitmore would provide additional details about the family's history, while Lisa, Daniel, and Emily would be responsible for organizing and presenting the information in an accessible manner.

As the group worked on documentation, they also began to consider the future of the mansion. With the dark pact undone and the negative energy dissipating, the mansion was in a position to be restored and used in a positive way. Lisa suggested that they could turn the mansion into a center for research and education on esoteric history and ancient practices.

The idea of transforming the mansion into a place of knowledge and learning resonated with everyone. "The mansion has been a place of darkness and mystery for so long. Turning it into an educational center could be a way to give it a new purpose and ensure that the history and knowledge we have discovered is not lost," Lisa said.

Daniel and Emily were enthusiastic about the idea. "We could host events and talks about esoteric history, ancient rituals, and the truth behind dark covenants. We could also offer workshops and classes for those interested in learning more about these topics," Daniel suggested.

Dr. Whitmore, though initially reticent, realized that the proposal offered a positive way to use his family's mansion and legacy. "I am willing to support this idea. The mansion can be a place of learning and growth rather than a symbol of darkness. I'm committed to helping in any way I can."

With the support of Dr. Whitmore, the group began planning to transform the mansion into a research and education center. Meetings were organized and contacts were established with experts in esoteric history and ancient practices to collaborate on the project.

Over the next few weeks, the group worked restoring the mansion and creating the school. Lisa and Daniel were in charge of the organization and planning of the events and workshops, while Emily focused on the documentation and collection of historical information.

Dr. Whitmore was also actively involved in the project, providing details about the family's history and helping to ensure that the mansion became a place of knowledge and learning. As the school began to take shape, the group felt more hopeful and motivated to continue their mission.

Eventually, the Whitmore mansion was opened as a center for research and education on esoteric history and ancient practices. The opening of the center was a significant event that attracted experts, researchers, and enthusiasts from all over the world. The mansion, once a place of darkness and mystery, had been transformed into a beacon of knowledge and understanding.

Lisa, Daniel, and Emily were proud of what they had accomplished. The restoration of the mansion and the creation of the educational center represented a new beginning and an opportunity to share knowledge and lessons learned with the world.

Dr. Whitmore, pleased with the result, thanked the group for their dedication and effort. "They have done an incredible job. The mansion now serves a positive purpose and my family's legacy has been restored in a significant way."

Lisa smiled and nodded. "It was a long road, but it was worth it. Now, we have the opportunity to make a difference and ensure that the history and insights we have discovered are valued and understood."

With the school up and running and the Whitmore family legacy restored, the group prepared to face the future with optimism. The mansion, now a symbol of knowledge and learning, offered new opportunities to explore and discover. Lisa, Daniel, and Emily were ready to move on and face any new challenges that might arise.

Chapter 20

The research and education center on esoteric history and ancient practices at the Whitmore mansion had begun to attract the attention of experts and enthusiasts from all over the world. Lisa, Daniel, and Emily were immersed in their work, helping to organize events, workshops, and talks that covered a wide range of topics related to esoteric history. Dr. Whitmore was also involved, offering his knowledge of his family's history and contributing to the center's activities.

One day, while going through old documents for an upcoming presentation, Lisa found an old diary hidden among the archives. The diary was covered in dust and seemed to have been there for many years. Upon opening it, he discovered that it was written by an ancestor of the Whitmore family who had been deeply involved in the creation of the dark covenant. The diary contained detailed entries about the rituals, the decisions made, and the motivations behind the pact.

Lisa decided that the diary should be examined carefully. He called Daniel and Emily to share his finding and discuss the next step. Daniel joined Lisa at the downtown library, where Emily was organizing the documents for the upcoming exhibition.

"I found this diary in the archives. It seems to be from someone who was at the heart of the dark covenant," Lisa said as she placed the diary on the table.

Emily looked up from her work and walked over. "What's in the diary?"

Lisa began to read aloud the first entries. The journal talked about the creation of the covenant, the promises made, and the sacrifices made to gain power and control. As I read, it became apparent that the covenant had been more complex and darker than they had imagined.

"This journal provides details about an aspect of the covenant that we haven't seen before," Lisa said. "It speaks of a secret clause that was added to the covenant and that was not mentioned in any other document."

Daniel frowned as he listened. "What secret clause?"

Lisa continued reading. The clause mentioned a "hidden spring" that could activate a final phase of the pact if certain conditions were not met. According to the newspaper, this final phase was a control mechanism that could be released in case attempts to break the pact failed or were insufficient.

"The secret clause appears to be a measure of last resort to ensure that the pact is never completely undone," Lisa explained. "If the pact is not treated with care, this final phase could be activated and cause chaos and destruction."

Emily looked at Lisa with concern. "That sounds dangerous. If this clause is triggered, we could face even bigger problems."

The group decided to investigate further to determine if the secret clause had been activated or if there were any associated risks. They gathered all the relevant documents and began to search for any indication that the control mechanism might have been released.

While going through the documents, Daniel discovered a series of symbols in the files that appeared to be related to the secret clause. The symbols were complex and related to rituals of high magic and control. Apparently, the covenant had a built-in defense system to protect against being completely undone.

Lisa, Daniel, and Emily prepared to conduct one last exam at the mansion to make sure there wasn't any activation of the secret clause. They headed to the oldest and darkest areas of the mansion, looking for signs of unusual activity or residual energy.

While investigating, the group noticed subtle changes in the atmosphere of the mansion. Some areas seemed to have been affected by a dark presence, and the energy in the place was becoming denser and denser. Lisa felt a chill run down her spine as she sensed the presence of an energy that hadn't been there before.

The group made their way to the underground hall, the place where they had performed the final ritual. Upon arrival, they found the atmosphere in the hall to be especially tense. The air was charged and the altar seemed to vibrate with an unsettling energy.

Lisa began to examine the altar and the esoteric objects they had used in the final ritual. Upon inspecting the symbols and crystal spheres, he noticed that some of the symbols had changed and seemed to be resonating with a dark energy.

"It looks like the control mechanism may have been activated," Lisa said with concern. "We need to act quickly to neutralize any residual effects."

Daniel and Emily helped Lisa prepare a new ritual to counter the secret clause. They used the documents found in the diary and esoteric symbols to create a ritual of protection and restoration. The goal was to ensure that the dark covenant and the secret clause would not cause further harm.

The group began the ritual, reciting the words of power and using the esoteric objects to channel the energy. As they advanced, the atmosphere in the hall began to change. The dark energy seemed to slowly dissipate and the atmosphere became calmer.

Finally, the ritual came to its conclusion and the group felt a sense of relief. The atmosphere in the underground hall had calmed down and the dark energy had disappeared. Lisa, Daniel, and Emily were exhausted but satisfied that they had handled the situation.

Dr. Whitmore, who had been waiting outside, approached the group with a worried but hopeful expression. "Is everything okay?"

Lisa nodded, smiling with relief. "Yes, we have neutralized the secret clause and ensured that the dark pact does not cause any more problems. We can now be confident that the Whitmore family legacy has been fully restored."

Dr. Whitmore took a deep breath, grateful for the group's effort. "I am indebted to you. They have faced significant challenges and have ensured a positive future for the mansion and for my family's history."

With the situation finally resolved, the group felt relieved and optimistic about the future. The Whitmore mansion, now free of dark influences and with a renewed purpose, offered a new horizon to explore and discover. The school would continue its mission of sharing knowledge and lessons learned, and the Whitmore family's legacy would be remembered in a positive and constructive way.

Lisa, Daniel, and Emily prepared to move on with their lives, grateful for the opportunity to have faced and overcome the challenge of the dark pact. With the future full of possibilities and hope, they were ready to face any new challenges that might arise and continue their mission of promoting knowledge and understanding.

Chapter 21

The Whitmore mansion continued to function as a vibrant center of research and education. Its transformation from a place of darkness and mystery to a beacon of knowledge and understanding had been a success, and the positive impact on the community had been significant. Lisa, Daniel, and Emily were pleased with the results, but a new series of events began to develop an additional layer of intrigue and challenge.

One morning, Lisa received a package without a return address at her downtown office. The package was small, wrapped in brown paper without any labels, and contained only one object: an antique key with an intricate design. Next to the key was a handwritten note that read, "To unlock what is still hidden."

Lisa, intrigued, showed the key and note to Daniel and Emily. "I have no idea who sent this or what it may open, but the message suggests that there is something else we need to discover."

"There seem to be more secrets hidden in the mansion," Emily commented, looking at the key with interest. "Perhaps there is a part of the mansion that we haven't fully explored."

They decided to investigate to determine what could unlock the key. The mansion was sprawling and full of secret corners, and they had already found several hidden spaces during their investigation. With the key in hand, they began to go through the old plans and files in search of possible places that the key could open.

After a few hours of searching, Daniel found a reference to a small office hidden in a corner of the basement, described in one of the old documents as a place that had been sealed as a precaution. The description matched the design of the key.

The group headed to the basement to explore the hidden office. When they arrived, they found a door hidden behind a wooden panel. Lisa inserted the key into the lock and slowly turned it. With a click, the door opened, revealing a small, dusty room.

Inside the office, they found a series of documents and old objects. There were shelves full of books, wooden boxes, and an old dust-covered desk. Lisa and the group began to examine the contents of the dispatch, looking for clues as to its purpose and any connection to the dark pact.

Among the objects, they found a leather-bound book with the title "The Echoes of the Past." The book appeared to be a chronicle of historical events and rituals associated with the Whitmore family, which had not been documented in previous archives. Upon opening the book, they discovered that it contained details about additional rituals and aspects of the dark covenant that had never been revealed before.

Lisa began to read aloud the passages of the book. "It appears that this book details rituals that were performed to keep the covenant in check and ensure that the secret clause was not activated. It also mentions a secret group within the Whitmore family that oversaw and maintained the pact."

The book included details about a secret network of followers and protectors of the covenant, who had worked in the shadows to ensure that the covenant was not broken. The followers were known as "The Custodians of the Legacy" and had a crucial role in protecting and maintaining the covenant.

"This changes everything we thought we knew," Daniel said, as he read a passage about the Guardians of the Legacy. "It seems that there was an organized structure to keep the pact and its secrets, even after an attempt was made to undo it."

Emily reviewed the additional documents in the office and found a series of letters and notes detailing the activities of the Legacy Custodians. The letters included instructions on how to ensure the pact remained in check and how to handle any potential threats.

"These documents suggest that the Legacy Custodians were prepared to deal with any attempt to break the covenant," Emily said. "It could be that there are still active followers of this group who are trying to protect the pact or who are seeking to regain their power."

The group decided that they needed to investigate further to understand the current influence of the Legacy Custodians and how they might be involved in the current situation. The revelation of this secret group introduced a new layer of complexity to their investigation and raised new questions about the goals and motivations of the Custodians.

Lisa, Daniel, and Emily began searching for clues to the current existence of the Legacy Custodians. They reviewed the ancient documents and looked for contacts in the esoteric community who might have information about the group. They also considered the possibility that some of the dark covenant's followers might still be active and looking to regain lost power.

As they continued their investigation, the group began to receive disturbing signals. They realized that there were sabotage attempts at the school, with documents and files manipulated and esoteric objects mysteriously disappearing. The situation seemed to indicate that someone was trying to interfere with their work and keep the secrets they were uncovering hidden.

Dr. Whitmore, upon learning of the problems, was concerned but determined to help. "It is evident that we are touching on a delicate issue. The Guardians of the Legacy may be trying to protect their secrets and influence. We need to be careful and move forward with caution."

Lisa nodded. "We must find out who the Legacy Custodians are and what they want before it causes more trouble. This could be more complicated than we thought."

With a new mission in mind, the group continued their investigation, facing challenges and obstacles as they unraveled the hidden secrets of the Whitmore family. The hidden dispatch and the book "The Echoes of the Past" had opened a new window into the family's dark past, and Lisa, Daniel, and Emily were determined to unravel the truth and ensure that the Whitmore family's legacy was preserved fairly and fully.

Chapter 22

The revelation of the Legacy Custodians and the discovery of the hidden office in Whitmore Manor had intensified the group's investigation. Lisa, Daniel, and Emily were more determined than ever to uncover the truth behind the secret group that had overseen the dark pact and its rituals. The sabotage at the school also added to the urgency of its mission.

Night fell on the mansion, and the group gathered in the library to plan their next step. Lisa and Daniel were going through the documents found in the hidden office, while Emily investigated possible connections to other esoteric groups.

"We must find the Legacy Custodians before they find a way to sabotage our work further," Lisa said, determinedly. "The documents suggest that they have been operating in the shadows for a long time, and could be seeking to regain control of the pact."

Daniel nodded. "The key is in the documents and letters we found. Maybe there are specific names, places, or rituals that we can track down to find these Custodians."

Emily looked up from her research. "I have found some references in esoteric texts to secret groups and occult societies that could be related to the Custodians of Legacy. It might be helpful to investigate these groups to see if they have any connection to the Whitmore family."

The group decided that their next step would be to explore these connections and try to identify potential current members of the Legacy Custodians. They knew they had to proceed cautiously, as the risk of facing a secret group with dark intentions was high.

The next day, Lisa, Daniel, and Emily headed to a bookstore specializing in esoteric texts and the occult. The bookstore, called "The Arcane Corner," was known for its unique collection of rare books and ancient documents related to esoteric practices. Its owner, Mr. Jonathan Blackwood, was an expert in the field and could have valuable information.

Mr. Blackwood, a middle-aged man with an enigmatic appearance, greeted them at the store. "Welcome. How can I help you today?"

Lisa briefly explained her situation and mentioned her interest in secret groups and occult societies. "We are looking for information about a group called the Custodians of Legacy. We think they could be related to the Whitmore family and the dark pact."

Mr. Blackwood frowned and nodded slowly. "I've heard rumors about a group with that name. The Legacy Custodians were known for maintaining the balance of certain dark rituals and secrets. Even though I don't have much in my files, I can search my logs and see if I find anything relevant."

While Mr. Blackwood was going through the files, the group scoured the library for clues. Emily found a book titled "Secret Societies and Occult Magic," which contained information about groups similar to the Legacy Custodians. The book mentioned a network of secret societies that had influenced esoteric history and how they maintained their anonymity.

Daniel joined Emily with a book titled "The Power of Lost Rites." This book contained details about ancient rituals and how secret groups could operate to preserve their secrets and power. Some of the rituals described seemed to match the details they had found in the hidden office.

Mr. Blackwood returned with a folder of old documents. "I have found some references to the Guardians of Legacy in my records. It seems that they were known for their ability to keep secrets and protect dark rituals. Here are some mentions of their activities and contacts."

Lisa and Daniel reviewed the documents, which contained references to secret meeting places, names of contacts, and symbols associated with the Legacy Custodians. Some of the names in the documents were familiar, as they appeared in the letters found in the hidden office.

"These documents seem to confirm that the Legacy Custodians may still be active," Daniel commented, as he reviewed a list of names and locations. "Some of these contacts could be involved in the sabotage we have experienced."

Lisa nodded. "We need to continue investigating these contacts and see if we can find any links to the recent incidents at the school. We must also be prepared for any confrontation that may arise."

The group thanked Mr. Blackwood for his help and left the bookstore with the new information. They decided to split up to investigate the contacts mentioned in the documents and look for any evidence of the activity of the Legacy Custodians.

Lisa and Daniel headed to one of the locations mentioned in the documents, an old building on the outskirts of town that appeared to have been used as a secret meeting place. Emily stayed at the mansion to continue investigating and try to identify possible followers of the group.

The building Lisa and Daniel arrived at was in a state of disrepair and appeared to have been abandoned for a long time. However, documents indicated that the site could still have connections to the Legacy Custodians.

While exploring the building, they found several esoteric symbols etched into the walls and some ancient objects that appeared to be related to rituals. They also found a number of documents confirming that the place had been used for secret meetings.

"This appears to be an ancient meeting place for the Custodians of the Legacy," Lisa said, as she reviewed the documents found. "It could be that they still use this place for their activities."

Daniel found a hidden entrance in one of the walls, which led to an underground basement. Upon descending, they discovered a hidden space filled with more documents, esoteric objects, and symbols related to the dark covenant.

"This place confirms that the Legacy Custodians have been operating in the shadows," Daniel said. "We have to make sure that this web of secrets doesn't interfere with our work anymore."

Meanwhile, Emily continued to investigate the mansion and found more clues about the group's possible followers. He discovered that some people in the esoteric community had shown interest in recent events and might be connected to the Legacy Custodians.

The group met again to discuss their findings. The information gathered confirmed that the Legacy Custodians were still active and that they might be attempting to regain lost power. Lisa, Daniel, and Emily were determined to move forward with their mission and ensure that the Whitmore family's legacy remained protected.

With the secret network of the Legacy Custodians discovered and the meeting places identified, the group prepared to face the challenges that awaited them. They knew that they would have to face a group that had operated in the shadows for a long time, and they were ready to uncover the truth and protect the future of the Whitmore mansion.

Chapter 23

Lisa, Daniel, and Emily's investigation into the Legacy Custodians was taking a new direction. The secret network had begun to crumble, revealing more information about followers and meeting places. The group knew they had to act cautiously, but also quickly, to avoid any further damage and protect the Whitmore family's legacy.

After discovering the former meeting place of the Legacy Custodians and clues to their current activities, Lisa decided it was time to make a decisive move. He met with Daniel and Emily in the library to discuss the next step.

"We have enough information to start asking tough questions," Lisa said, as she went through the documents they had found in the basement of the old building. "We know that the Legacy Custodians are active and that they could be involved in sabotage at the school. We must confront them directly to prevent them from interfering further."

Daniel nodded. "We could try to trace some of the contacts mentioned in the documents. We may be able to uncover their plans and stop any harmful activity before it's too late."

Emily agreed. "We can also use the information we find to strengthen security at the mansion and the school. We need to be prepared for any confrontation."

The group decided to split up to address several fronts: Lisa and Daniel would be in charge of tracking down contacts and possible members of the Legacy Custodians, while Emily would focus on reinforcing security at the mansion and the educational center.

Lisa and Daniel began their research in the city, visiting the locations mentioned in the ancient documents. One of the addresses they found led them to an office building in an industrial area of the city. The place seemed to be a front for darker activities.

Upon entering the building, Lisa and Daniel found a deserted reception and a hallway that led to several offices. They decided to explore the offices in search of clues. While reviewing the archives and documents, they found a series of communications confirming the presence of active members of the Legacy Custodians.

"These documents show that there are meetings scheduled at a specific location," Daniel said, pointing to a calendar with dates and addresses written down. "It could be our chance to confront the Custodians and discover their plans."

With the information in hand, Lisa and Daniel headed to the location of the next meeting, which was in a secluded warehouse on the outskirts of town. The place appeared to be in an industrial area, surrounded by deserted and dark buildings.

Upon arriving at the warehouse, the group prepared for what could be a confrontation. The main entrance was locked with a lock, but Daniel found a secondary entrance that appeared to be a way to access the interior without being detected.

"We must be cautious," Lisa whispered, as she opened the secondary entrance. "We don't know how many Legacy Custodians might be here."

The group entered the warehouse and moved silently through the shadows. The place was filled with boxes and building materials, which provided good cover. Lisa and Daniel made their way toward an area where murmurs and footsteps could be heard.

As they approached, they saw a group of people gathered in a back room, arguing in low voices. The group seemed to consist of several masked and hooded figures, and in the center was a table with documents and esoteric objects.

Lisa and Daniel hid behind some boxes and overheard the conversation. One of the members of the group, a man with a deep, authoritative voice, was talking about an upcoming ritual they planned to perform to strengthen the dark pact and regain lost control.

"This ritual is our last chance to restore the power of the covenant," the man said. "We must ensure that the school and the Whitmore mansion do not interfere with our plans. If we fail to complete the ritual, we will lose our influence forever."

Lisa and Daniel realized that the group was planning to perform a crucial ritual that could have serious consequences. They knew they had to act quickly to prevent the ritual from taking place.

While they were preparing their intervention, Emily at the mansion was also working to reinforce security. He had installed additional security cameras and placed protective barriers around key areas. However, the sabotage continued, with some equipment being tampered with and altered without explanation.

Emily was checking the security cameras when she noticed a suspicious figure in one of the images. The figure seemed to be attempting to enter the mansion from an unforeseen point. Emily decided she should investigate and prepared to face any threats that might arise.

Back at the warehouse, Lisa and Daniel prepared to confront the Legacy Custodians. They moved carefully to approach the group undetected. As they were about to disrupt the meeting, the group of Custodians began to perform the ritual, lighting candles and reciting words in an ancient language.

"Now is the time," Lisa whispered, as they prepared to intervene. "We must stop this ritual before it is too late."

Lisa and Daniel advanced towards the group and, with a quick movement, interrupted the ritual. The room erupted in chaos as the Legacy's Custodians turned to them in surprise and anger.

"Stop!" ordered Lisa, as she walked over to the table and collected the documents and esoteric objects. "The ritual is stopped. We will not allow them to continue with their plans."

The Legacy Custodians tried to resist, but Lisa and Daniel were prepared to face them. A tense confrontation ensued in which Lisa and Daniel had to fight off the group members who tried to stop them.

Meanwhile, at the mansion, Emily managed to intercept the suspicious figure and discovered that he was one of the followers of the Legacy Custodians who was trying to sabotage the new security measures. Emily managed to stop the intruder and secure the area.

The confrontation in the warehouse continued, and Lisa and Daniel fought with determination to ensure that the ritual was not completed. With the help of some of the esoteric objects they had found, they managed to neutralize the Legacy Custodians and dismantle the ritual.

The group of Custodians of the Legacy was captured and handed over to the authorities. Lisa, Daniel, and Emily were exhausted but relieved. They had averted a potential disaster and dismantled a significant portion of the secret network.

With the Legacy Custodians disabled and security beefed up at the mansion and school, the group prepared to face the next challenge. They knew that there were still more secrets to be uncovered and that the Whitmore family's legacy needed to be protected with constant vigilance.

Chapter 24

After the confrontation in the warehouse and the capture of the Legacy Custodians, Lisa, Daniel, and Emily took a brief breather, but the sense of urgency hadn't diminished. Despite having dismantled a significant portion of the secret network, there were still unanswered questions and a lingering sense of unease in the air.

The Whitmore mansion had regained its calm atmosphere, but Lisa couldn't shake the feeling that there was something more she had to discover. During the investigation and confrontation, several esoteric documents and objects had been recovered, and one of those documents seemed to contain crucial information that they had not yet deciphered.

That morning, Lisa, Daniel, and Emily met in the mansion's library to examine the remaining documents and plan their next steps. The atmosphere in the room was one of concentration and determination. Lisa spread out an old scroll she had found in the warehouse on the table.

"This scroll appears to be some sort of map or guide," Lisa said, pointing to the intricate symbols and writings on the document. "We haven't had a chance to analyze it in detail, but I think it might contain a final clue about the dark covenant or the Legacy Custodians."

Daniel looked at the scroll carefully. "The symbols seem to have a specific pattern. It could be a map that leads to some important place. We need to decipher it to understand what it is telling us."

Emily, who had been going through the esoteric objects found in the warehouse, found a book titled "The Secrets of the Hidden Legacy." The book contained descriptions of various ancient symbols and rituals, and some of them matched those that appeared on the scroll.

"This book could help us interpret the symbols on the scroll," Emily suggested. "Let's see if we can find any correspondence."

Lisa, Daniel, and Emily immersed themselves in the book and the scroll, working together to decipher the symbols and text. After several hours of analysis, they managed to identify a set of symbols that represented a series of locations and objects.

"The scroll seems to indicate a number of key locations that are related to the dark covenant and the Guardians of Legacy," Lisa explained. "If we follow these clues, we might uncover the latest enigma that has been eluding us."

The locations mentioned on the scroll included locations in both the mansion and the surrounding city. Lisa and Daniel decided to investigate the places near the mansion first, while Emily would be in charge of tracking down the locations in the city.

The first location was a hidden garden on the grounds of the mansion, an area that had been neglected and almost forgotten. Lisa and Daniel headed to the garden and began to explore. Among the plants and dense foliage, they found a series of stones and statues that seemed to be aligned according to the scroll's pattern.

"These stones seem to form a pattern that matches the map on the scroll," Daniel said, as he examined the stones. "There's a statue in the center that seems to be the focal point."

Lisa approached the statue and discovered a series of hidden inscriptions at the base. Using the symbol book, they were able to interpret the inscriptions, which revealed a series of coordinates and a warning about a forbidden ritual.

"This confirms that there is a connection between the garden and the dark covenant," Lisa said. "It seems that the garden has been used for some kind of secret ritual or ceremony in the past."

The next location on the scroll led them to a cave on the outskirts of the city, a place that seemed to be related to the ritual mentioned in the symbol book. Lisa and Daniel headed to the cave, carrying exploration equipment and flashlights with them.

The cave was dark and damp, and appeared to have been used as a meeting or ceremony place. Inside the cave, they found a series of markings on the walls and a central altar with esoteric symbols. The altar seemed to be set up for a ritual and had several ancient objects arranged on it.

"This place has been used for important rituals," Daniel observed. "We must be careful. There may still be elements related to the dark covenant."

Lisa examined the altar and found a box hidden under a stone. The box was decorated with symbols that matched those on the scroll. Inside the box, they found a set of documents and an ancient amulet.

"These documents appear to be records of rituals and covenants made by the Custodians of the Legacy," Lisa said, as she reviewed the papers. "The amulet seems to be an object of power that could be related to the covenant."

While Lisa and Daniel investigated the cave, Emily was in town, scouting the remaining locations. He found an old bookstore hidden in an alley that seemed to be related to the dark pact. The bookstore was full of rare books and old documents.

Emily found a book titled "The Secrets of the Pactum Obscura," which contained detailed information about rituals and esoteric objects related to the covenant. The book mentioned a final ritual that was performed to ensure the permanence of the covenant and the loyalty of its followers.

Returning to the mansion, the group gathered to discuss the findings. The documents found in the cave and the book discovered by Emily seemed to indicate that the dark pact had been designed to last indefinitely, with periodic rituals to maintain its influence.

"This seems to be the ultimate enigma," Lisa said, showing the documents and the amulet. "The dark covenant is designed to be eternal, with rituals to ensure its perpetuity. We must find a way to neutralize these rituals and ensure that the pact does not threaten the Whitmore family again."

The group prepared to perform a final ritual to deactivate the dark covenant and ensure that it could not be reactivated. They would use the information and objects they had recovered to perform the ritual safely.

Night was approaching, and the group headed to the key locations identified on the scroll to perform the ritual. With the help of the amulet and documents, Lisa, Daniel, and Emily carried out the final ritual, ensuring that the dark pact was neutralized.

At the end of the ritual, the group felt a palpable relief. The dark pact, which had caused so much chaos and mystery, had been deactivated, and the Whitmore family was finally free from the influence of the Legacy Custodians.

With the pact neutralized and the secret network dismantled, Lisa, Daniel, and Emily were satisfied with the outcome of their investigation. The Whitmore mansion and school were now protected, and the family's legacy had been secured for the future.

Chapter 25

Calm seemed to have returned to the Whitmore mansion after the deactivation of the dark pact. Lisa, Daniel, and Emily were relieved, but they knew that the impact of their discoveries and actions would still resonate in their lives. Although the immediate danger had been neutralized, the weight of what they had learned was still present.

The first light of day filtered through the windows of the mansion, and the group gathered in the library to reflect on their recent discoveries. Emily had been going through the documents found in the last ritual, while Lisa and Daniel were busy organizing the evidence and ensuring that all esoteric objects were safely stored.

"Now that we've deactivated the pact, we need to consider how to proceed," Lisa said, as she examined a copy of the documents. "We cannot allow history to repeat itself. We must ensure that these secrets do not fall into the wrong hands."

Daniel nodded, checking the ancient amulet. "The information we find in the documents and the book about the dark covenant is important. We should consider sharing this information with authorities or experts in the field to ensure it is kept under control."

Emily, who had been in contact with some academics and experts in esotericism, intervened. "I've been talking to a couple of historians who are interested in the esoteric legacy of the Whitmore family. It might be helpful to share the information with them so they can help preserve knowledge appropriately."

While discussing these issues, Emily received a phone call. It was Mr. Jonathan Blackwood, the owner of the bookstore "The Arcane Corner."

"Lisa, Daniel, Emily, I must speak to you urgently," Blackwood said, his tone grave. "I have received information that could change the way we understand the dark covenant and the Guardians of Legacy. The documents I found in my bookstore seem to have a deeper connection to the Whitmore family's past."

Lisa and Daniel looked at each other curiously. "What kind of information?" asked Lisa.

"It's something I can't explain over the phone," Blackwood replied. "I need you to come to the bookstore to show you what I've found. It's crucial to completing our investigation."

The group headed to the "Arcane Corner" bookstore, where they met Blackwood. The bookstore owner greeted them with a worried expression and led them to a private room at the back of the store.

"In my old records, I have found a set of documents that appear to be linked to an important historical event in the Whitmore family," Blackwood explained. "These documents indicate that the dark covenant was not an isolated creation, but part of a much larger and more complex legacy."

Blackwood showed Lisa, Daniel, and Emily a series of ancient scrolls and letters, some of which were written in an ancient language. "These documents appear to be records of rituals and covenants made by the Whitmore family over the centuries. There are references to historical events and prominent figures that could have influenced the development of the covenant."

Lisa examined the documents carefully. "These records appear to be a detailed chronology of the Whitmore family's influence and its connection to the dark covenant. What implications might these findings have?"

"It seems that the dark covenant and the Legacy Custodians have been present in the history of the Whitmore family for generations," Blackwood explained. "These documents indicate that the family has been part of a wider network of secret societies and dark rituals. The dark covenant was not just an isolated event, but part of an ongoing pattern."

Daniel went through one of the scrolls and noticed a number of names and dates that seemed to coincide with important historical events. "These documents appear to be connected to influential historical figures and key events. This could imply that the dark pact has had a significant impact on history."

Blackwood nodded. "Exactly. Most disturbingly, there are indications that the pact may not have been completely deactivated. There are mentions of periodic rituals to maintain the covenant's influence, suggesting that there could be more to it than what we've seen so far."

Emily looked at the documents with concern. "If the pact has not been completely deactivated, we could face more problems in the future. We need to investigate further and ensure that the Whitmore family's legacy is not a threat again."

The group decided that their next step would be to investigate the historical connections and events mentioned in the documents. Blackwood offered to help, as he had access to historical records and archives that could provide more insight into the impact of the Whitmore family and the dark covenant.

As they worked together to decipher the documents and trace historical events, the group realized that their research was unearthing more secrets than they expected. Historical records revealed a fascinating but disturbing history of the Whitmore family and their influence on the past.

Lisa, Daniel, and Emily immersed themselves in the research, exploring ancient archives and consulting with historical experts. They discovered that the Whitmore family had been involved in a number of dark events and rituals over the centuries, many of which were related to the preservation of the dark covenant.

Meanwhile, the Whitmore family's legacy continued to be a source of mystery and fascination. The group's findings provided a new perspective on the family's history and its connections to secret societies and esoteric rituals.

The group was determined to complete their investigation and ensure that the dark pact and associated secrets were completely disabled. They knew that there were still more puzzles to be solved and that the impact of their work would continue to resonate in the future.

The investigation continued, and the group worked tirelessly to uncover the truth behind the Whitmore family's dark legacy. Although the road ahead was uncertain, they were determined to protect the future and ensure that the family's legacy was understood and treated with the respect it deserved.

Chapter 26

The group was increasingly immersed in the complex web of secrets and mysteries surrounding the Whitmore family's dark legacy. After the recent discoveries in Jonathan Blackwood's bookstore, a new dimension had opened up in his research. Historical documents and ancient records revealed that the dark pact had been part of a larger network of secret societies and esoteric rituals throughout history.

Lisa, Daniel, and Emily had committed themselves to deciphering all the secrets, determined to ensure that the Whitmore family's legacy would not pose a threat in the future. The next step in his research was to discover the real purpose behind the rituals and the impact they had had on history.

Early in the morning, the group met in the library of the Whitmore Mansion. The atmosphere was one of concentration and expectation as they prepared the documents, parchments, and books for analysis. Lisa had spent the night going through the historical records they had found in the bookstore and identified patterns that might be crucial to understanding the purpose of the dark pact.

"What we've found so far suggests that the dark covenant has deep connections to significant historical events," Lisa began, placing a historical map on the table. "The documents indicate that the Whitmore family has been involved in key moments in history, and these rituals were meant to preserve their influence."

Daniel and Emily nodded as they reviewed the map and related documents. Daniel pointed to several historical locations that coincided with events mentioned in the documents. "These locations are tied to prominent historical figures and events that marked the course of history. It seems that the dark pact has been at play at crucial moments."

Emily, who had been reviewing the book "The Secrets of the Pactum Obscura," found a passage that spoke of a final ceremony to consolidate the power of the covenant. "This book mentions a final ritual that is performed to ensure the loyalty of the followers and the perpetuity of the covenant. This may explain why the covenant has persisted over time."

Lisa, reading the passage carefully, added: "The final ritual seems to have a very powerful symbolic component. It could be related to a specific object or place that acts as an anchor for the covenant. We need to identify that object or place."

The group decided that their next task would be to track down the objects or places mentioned in the historical documents. One place in particular had caught his eye: an old mansion on the outskirts of the city that, according to documents, had been used in the past for ceremonies related to the dark pact.

The mansion, known as the Villa Ravenscroft, was an imposing building surrounded by crumbling gardens and ruined structures. Although it had been abandoned for decades, it still maintained an aura of mystery. Lisa, Daniel, and Emily headed to Ravenscroft Villa, hoping to find clues that could reveal the truth behind the dark pact.

Upon arriving at the mansion, the group noticed that the structure was in a state of disrepair, but it still retained an eerie majesty. The atmosphere was gloomy and silent, and the overgrown vegetation around the mansion gave a sense of abandonment. Lisa used a flashlight to light the way as they entered through a back door that had been forced.

The mansion was full of dust and cobwebs, but Lisa, Daniel, and Emily moved carefully so as not to disturb anything unnecessarily. They began to explore the rooms and hallways, looking for any clues that might be related to the dark pact.

In the west wing of the mansion, they found a room hidden behind a false wall. Inside the hall, there were a number of ancient objects, including a stone altar and a number of esoteric artifacts. The altar was covered with symbols and runes that matched those on the scroll found in the warehouse.

"This is exactly what we were looking for," Lisa said, as she examined the altar and the objects around it. "It seems that this place was used to perform important rituals related to the dark covenant."

Daniel found a chest hidden under the altar. Inside the chest were several documents and a medallion-shaped object, adorned with the same symbols found in historical records and the scroll.

"This medallion must be the anchor object mentioned in the documents," Daniel said, as he examined the medallion. "It could be the key to understanding the final ritual and purpose of the dark covenant."

Emily went through the documents found in the chest and found a manuscript that described a ritual of consolidating power, very similar to the one mentioned in the book "The Secrets of the Pactum Obscura." The manuscript detailed the steps to perform the final ritual, which included summoning dark entities and creating a lasting bond with the covenant.

"This manuscript confirms that the medallion and altar are essential to the final ritual," Emily explained. "The ritual is performed to ensure that the covenant endures and that the influence of the Legacy Custodians is maintained."

With this new information, the group realized that they had the opportunity to completely deactivate the dark pact. The medallion and altar were key to completing the final ritual safely, and in doing so, they could ensure that the covenant could not be reactivated.

Lisa, Daniel, and Emily prepared to perform the final ritual at Ravenscroft Villa, using the medallion and documents to guide them. The atmosphere in the mansion was tense and solemn as they prepared to perform the ritual.

With the objects and documents in hand, they began the final ritual at the stone altar. They used the symbols and words from the manuscript to carry out the process, making sure to follow each step precisely. The medallion was placed in the center of the altar, and symbols were traced around it.

While they were performing the ritual, the atmosphere in the mansion began to change. The sense of darkness and weight that had been present slowly dissipated, and a feeling of liberation began to fill the space.

Upon completing the ritual, the group felt a surge of relief. The dark pact had been completely deactivated, and the secrets that had plagued the Whitmore family for generations had finally been sealed.

Lisa, Daniel, and Emily left the mansion with a sense of accomplishment and satisfaction. They knew that they had completed their mission and that they had secured the future of the Whitmore family. The Villa Ravenscroft, now devoid of its dark influence, witnessed the conclusion of an important chapter in the family's history.

With the dark pact neutralized and secrets discovered, the group was ready to face the future with a new perspective. The legacy of the Whitmore family had been protected, and the echoes of the past had finally been silenced.

Chapter 27

Morning mist shrouded Whitmore Manor as Lisa, Daniel, and Emily returned from their last mission at Ravenscroft Villa. The atmosphere in the mansion was filled with a sense of renewed peace, but the investigation had not yet come to an end. Although they had deactivated the dark covenant and performed the final ritual, the historical documents and the manuscript discovered indicated that aspects of the dark legacy still remained to be resolved.

The group met in the library to discuss their next steps. Historical documents revealed details about an enigmatic figure known as the Custodian of the Legacy, a person who, according to legends, had the power to influence and control the dark pact and its followers. This figure seemed to be the latest enigma in the complex web of secrets they had unearthed.

"According to the documents, the Custodian of the Legacy is a key figure in the preservation of the dark covenant," Lisa explained, as she unfolded an ancient scroll on the table. "The text suggests that this person has the ability to manipulate the covenant and control its influence. If it's true, we need to identify who this person is and make sure they don't pose a threat."

Daniel went through the old records they had found in Ravenscroft Villa. "The Custodian of the Legacy appears to be a historical figure with significant influence on the Whitmore family. The documents mention that this person has been related to dark events throughout history."

Emily, who had been researching the historical connections and prominent figures, chimed in. "I have found references to several individuals who could have acted as Custodians of the Legacy at different times. We need to track down these figures and determine if any of them are still active today."

With this information, the group decided that their next task would be to investigate the identities and history of the potential Legacy Custodians. The research led them to explore historical archives and consult with experts in esoteric history.

One of the historical records revealed that the last known Legacy Custodian had been a man named Charles Whitmore, an ancestor of the Whitmore family who had mysteriously disappeared more than a century ago. According to the documents, Charles Whitmore had been the leader of a secret society tasked with maintaining the dark pact and had disappeared without a trace during a final ritual.

The group realized that finding information about Charles Whitmore could be crucial to understanding the potential threat of the Legacy Custodian. They decided to seek more details about his disappearance and any evidence that might indicate his whereabouts or subsequent activities.

The investigation led Lisa, Daniel, and Emily to an old archive in the city, where they found records about Charles Whitmore's disappearance. The documents indicated that Charles had been involved in a number of esoteric and ritual activities in a hidden mansion on the outskirts of the city, which appeared to be connected to the Villa Ravenscroft.

Determined to follow this lead, the group headed to the hidden mansion mentioned in the records. The mansion was an old, dilapidated building, similar to the Villa Ravenscroft, but with an even more oppressive atmosphere. The mansion was hidden in the middle of a dense forest, and the overgrown vegetation around it made the place seem forgotten by time.

Upon entering the mansion, the group found a space similar to the altar of the Villa Ravenscroft, with esoteric symbols and ancient artifacts. Lisa, Daniel, and Emily explored the rooms and found a number of documents and objects that appeared to be related to the dark rituals and legacy.

Among the documents, they found a diary that appeared to have belonged to Charles Whitmore. The diary contained writings and notes about his activities as Custodian of the Legacy, as well as details about rituals and esoteric objects. In the pages of the diary, Charles had written about his concern for the future of the dark covenant and his desire to ensure its perpetuity.

"This journal offers an in-depth insight into the mindset of the Legacy Custodian," Lisa commented, as she read Charles' notes. "It seems that he was obsessed with the dark pact and maintaining its influence."

Daniel found a map in the journal that indicated the location of a hidden place related to the covenant. "This map seems to point to a specific site that could be linked to the last ritual or to the preservation of the covenant."

Emily, who had been going through the objects found in the mansion, identified an amulet that matched the symbols in the diary. "This amulet could have been an object of power for Charles Whitmore, used in rituals to consolidate his control over the covenant."

The group decided that their next step would be to investigate the place marked on the map. The location was in a remote region of the forest, and the group prepared to head into the area in search of more clues.

After an arduous journey through the forest, they came to a hidden cave on a hill. The entrance to the cave was sealed with an ancient mechanism that appeared to have been designed to protect the interior. Lisa, Daniel, and Emily used the tracks from the diary to disable the mechanism and open the entrance.

Inside the cave, they found a series of chambers and underground passages. In one of the main chambers, there was an altar similar to that of the Villa Ravenscroft, but with a number of symbols and objects that seemed to be related to the final ritual of consolidating the covenant.

In the center of the chamber, they found an ancient sarcophagus that appeared to be sealed with magic and rituals. Documents in Charles' diary indicated that the sarcophagus contained the body of Charles Whitmore, which had been preserved in a state of suspended animation as part of a ritual to ensure the continuity of the covenant.

"This confirms that Charles Whitmore was the Custodian of the Legacy and that his body has been preserved as part of the dark covenant," Lisa said, as she examined the sarcophagus. "We must ensure that the sarcophagus is deactivated and that the dark legacy is completely sealed."

The group performed a final ritual in the chamber to deactivate the sarcophagus and ensure that the dark pact was completely neutralized. They used the diary documents and the amulet found in the hidden mansion to carry out the process.

With the ritual completed, the sarcophagus was deactivated, and the atmosphere in the cave became lighter and clearer. The dark covenant's influence was sealed, and the Legacy's Custodian, Charles Whitmore, was finally released from his state of suspended animation.

Lisa, Daniel, and Emily left the cave with a sense of accomplishment and relief. They had completed their mission and ensured that the dark legacy posed no threat to the Whitmore family or the future.

The group returned to the Whitmore mansion, where they reflected on the impact of their discoveries and the path traveled. The Whitmore family's dark legacy had been protected and defused, and the future looked brighter.

With the Legacy Custodian finally neutralized and the dark pact sealed, Lisa, Daniel, and Emily were ready to face the future with a new perspective. The history of the Whitmore family and its dark secrets had been unearthed and treated with the respect and attention they deserved.

Chapter 28

Lisa, Daniel, and Emily were in the library of the Whitmore mansion, going through the documents and objects they had found in the cave on the hill. Although they had disabled the dark covenant and neutralized the Legacy Custodian, they felt that there were still pieces of the puzzle to fit together.

Lisa placed an ancient book she'd found in the cave on the table, covered in dust and with a worn cover. "This book seems to be a kind of chronicle or guide about the dark covenant and the Guardians of Legacy. Perhaps it contains additional information that will help us better understand the legacy and its impact."

Daniel nodded and took the book carefully. "Let's examine it. If there's anything else we need to know, this book might contain the answers."

Emily, who had been reviewing the notes and related documents, looked at the texts carefully. "If the book has information about how the covenant has influenced different eras, it might give us an idea of how to prevent something similar from happening again."

Lisa and Daniel began reading the book while Emily went through the other documents. Reading the first few pages revealed a number of rituals and historical events related to the dark covenant, as well as details about the Legacy Custodians and their influence over time.

"The book mentions a key figure in the history of the covenant, a leader who has acted as an intermediary between the Custodians and the dark entities," Lisa said, pointing to a passage in the book. "This leader appears to have a crucial role in preserving and expanding the pact."

Emily, reading the same passage, added: "This leader could be someone who has been operating in the shadows to keep the pact active. If we can identify this person, we could prevent future problems."

Daniel found a passage in the book that spoke of a number of esoteric objects that were related to the dark covenant. "The book mentions a number of artifacts that have the power to influence the covenant and its rituals. We must ensure that these objects are located and secured."

While discussing these findings, they received an unexpected call from Jonathan Blackwood, the owner of the "Arcane Corner" bookstore. "Lisa, Daniel, Emily, I have important information that could change the course of our investigation. I need you to come to the bookstore as soon as possible."

The group headed to the bookstore immediately, eager to learn the new information. Upon arrival, Blackwood greeted them with a worried expression. "I have found a number of additional documents that could be related to the leader mentioned in the book. These documents suggest that the dark covenant's influence may not have completely ended."

"What kind of documents?" asked Lisa, as they made their way to a private room in the bookstore.

"They are records of a secret society that appears to have been operating in parallel to the Legacy Custodians," Blackwood explained. "These records indicate that the leader of the secret society has been working to preserve and expand the influence of the dark pact."

Blackwood showed Lisa, Daniel, and Emily a series of old documents containing information about the secret society and its leader. The records included details about rituals, secret meetings, and esoteric artifacts used by the society.

"The documents mention an individual named Elias Ravenscroft," Blackwood said. "It appears that he has been operating as the leader of the secret society and has been involved in activities related to the dark covenant."

The name Ravenscroft resonated with Lisa and Daniel. They recalled that the Ravenscroft Villa, where they had found the altar and medallion, was associated with influential figures in the history of the dark covenant.

"Elias Ravenscroft could be a crucial figure in preserving the covenant," Lisa said. "If we can find this person or discover their whereabouts, we could ensure that the dark legacy is completely neutralized."

The group decided that their next task would be to track down Elias Ravenscroft and determine his relationship to the dark pact. The documents indicated that Elias had been in contact with several members of the secret society and had performed rituals in different places.

The investigation led the group to search for clues about Elias Ravenscroft in historical archives and secret society records. They discovered that Elias had last been seen in a hidden mansion in the countryside, which appeared to be linked to the activities of the secret society.

With this new clue, the group headed to the mansion mentioned in the documents. The mansion was an ancient and majestic construction, surrounded by an overgrown garden. The atmosphere in the mansion was unsettling and gloomy, with a sense of abandonment and mystery.

While exploring the mansion, the group found a series of rooms and corridors that appeared to have been used for esoteric rituals. In one of the main rooms, they found an altar similar to that of the Ravenscroft Villa, but with symbols and objects that were related to the secret society's records.

Lisa, Daniel, and Emily searched the room and found a number of documents and objects that appeared to be related to Elias Ravenscroft's influence. Among the documents, they found a letter written by Elias that outlined his plans to expand the dark covenant's influence and maintain control over his followers.

"The letter reveals that Elias Ravenscroft was working to ensure that the dark covenant continued to be active and that his influence expanded," Lisa said. "It seems that he had a plan to revive the covenant and control the Legacy Custodians."

Daniel found a chest hidden in the room, which contained a number of esoteric artifacts and a medallion similar to the one they had found in the Ravenscroft Villa. "This medallion could have been used by Elijah to consolidate his power and control the dark pact."

Emily reviewed the documents and found a reference to a final ritual that Elias had planned to perform to ensure the perpetuity of the covenant. "This ritual seems to be similar to the one we perform at the Ravenscroft Villa. If we can neutralize this ritual, we could ensure that the dark covenant is completely deactivated."

The group decided to perform the final ritual at the mansion to ensure that the dark pact and Elias Ravenscroft's influence were completely neutralized. They used the documents and the medallion found in the mansion to carry out the process, following the steps outlined in Elias' letter.

With the ritual completed, the atmosphere in the mansion changed, and the influence of the dark pact dissipated. The group felt a surge of relief knowing that the dark legacy had been completely sealed and neutralized.

Lisa, Daniel, and Emily returned to the Whitmore mansion, where they reflected on the impact of their discoveries and the path they traveled. They had faced and overcome significant challenges to ensure that the dark legacy of the Whitmore family was protected.

With the Legacy Custodian neutralized and the dark covenant's influence deactivated, the group was ready to face the future with a new perspective. The legacy of the Whitmore family had been secured, and the dark secrets had finally been treated with the respect and attention they deserved.

Chapter 29

The sun was at its highest when Lisa, Daniel, and Emily returned to the Whitmore mansion after neutralizing Elias Ravenscroft's influence. Though they were relieved, the process of solving the dark riddles of the covenant had left a sense of unease that they could not ignore. They had succeeded in defusing the dark legacy, but connections to the past continued to beckon.

Lisa was in the library going through the final documents that had been brought from Ravenscroft Manor. "There's still something that doesn't quite fit," he remarked, handing Daniel and Emily an old genealogy book he'd found among Ravenscroft's objects. "There appear to be more details about the history of the Whitmore family and their relationship to the covenant."

Daniel examined the book carefully. "This book traces the Whitmore family's bloodlines and their connections to other influential families. There might be something else that helps us understand how the dark covenant has affected the family over the generations."

Emily joined the conversation. "The history of the Whitmore family is full of significant events, but there are also indications of dark events and rituals that could have influenced the present. If we can understand how these events have affected the family, we might find answers to some of the questions we still have."

While going through the book, they found a page that highlighted a number of important historical events related to the Whitmore family. Among them, there was a mention of an old family diary that had disappeared under mysterious circumstances. The diary appeared to contain crucial details about the history of the covenant and its influence on the family.

"The disappearance of this diary could be related to the dark events that we have been investigating," Lisa said. "If we can find this diary, we might uncover information that is still missing."

The group decided to investigate the disappearance of the family diary and trace its whereabouts. The research led them to contact historians and experts on the Whitmore family. They discovered that the diary had been recorded as lost during World War II, when the mansion had been occupied by invading forces and had suffered significant damage.

"It seems that the diary was lost in the chaotic events of the war," Daniel commented. "We must investigate the records of the time and look for clues as to what may have happened to the diary."

The investigation revealed that, during the war, the Whitmore mansion had been used as a base for secret operations and had suffered serious damage. Some documents indicated that several valuable objects and important records had been removed from the mansion prior to its occupation. Lisa, Daniel, and Emily began tracking these objects and records to determine if the diary had been taken elsewhere.

In the historical archives, they found a series of records about a covert operation carried out by a local resistance group. The group had been responsible for protecting and moving valuable objects and important documents out of the mansion during the occupation.

"It looks like the diary may have been taken to safety by this resistance group," Emily said, reviewing the records. "We need to track down the members of the resistance and find out if there is any information on the whereabouts of the diary."

The investigation led the group to contact descendants of resistance members who had participated in the operation. One of the descendants, an elderly man named Arthur Simmons, had vague memories of the operation and had preserved some documents related to the mission.

Arthur Simmons welcomed the group into his home, an old house on the outskirts of town. Although he was aged and frail, his memory was keen and his memories detailed. "I remember hearing about a diary that had been taken to safety," Arthur said, as he flipped through some old documents. "But I never knew what happened to him after the war."

Arthur shared with the group information about a warehouse in the camp where various objects and documents had been kept during the war. The warehouse had been sealed and forgotten after the war, and was thought to still contain valuable items.

The group decided to investigate the warehouse mentioned by Arthur. When they arrived, they found an old and dilapidated building, with an atmosphere of abandonment. Lisa, Daniel, and Emily began exploring the warehouse, looking for clues to the whereabouts of the family diary.

Among the objects and documents found in the warehouse, Lisa discovered a trunk sealed with security tapes and protective symbols. Upon opening the trunk, they found a number of old documents and books, including the family diary they had been looking for.

"This is the diary we've been looking for," Lisa said, with a mixture of relief and excitement. "We finally have a chance to find out what's in it."

The group reviewed the diary carefully. It contained a number of notes and accounts about the history of the dark covenant, as well as details about the events that had led to the covenant's influence on the Whitmore family. The diary revealed that the pact had been designed to protect the Whitmore family and secure their influence throughout history, but it had also come at a significant cost in terms of sacrifices and dark rituals.

"The diary provides a comprehensive look at how the compact has affected the Whitmore family over the generations," Emily said. "It seems that the pact has had a lasting impact on the family, even after our intervention."

Lisa, Daniel, and Emily realized that although they had neutralized the influence of the dark covenant, the impact of historical events still resonated with the Whitmore family. The diary was a testament to how the covenant had shaped the family's history and how the secrets of the past still resonated in the present.

With the diary in hand, the group returned to the Whitmore mansion to continue their research and reflect on the impact of their discoveries. They knew that although they had succeeded in defusing the dark pact, the history of the Whitmore family and its secrets continued to be part of their legacy.

The revelation of the diary provided them with a deeper understanding of the events that had shaped the dark legacy. Lisa, Daniel, and Emily were determined to protect the Whitmore family's future and ensure that echoes of the past would never again affect their lives.

Chapter 30

Lisa, Daniel, and Emily were at the Whitmore mansion, surrounded by the revelations that the Mirror of Truth had provided. They had uncovered crucial bits and pieces about the dark pact and its impact on the Whitmore family's history, but the sense that something still remained unresolved was still present.

With the mirror safely stored and the documents rearranged, the group made their way to the mansion's main office, where they sat around a table to discuss the mirror's visions. The images had shown not only ancient rituals, but also connections between the Whitmore family and a number of historical events related to the influence of the dark covenant.

Lisa was going through an old map she'd found in the trunk of the warehouse. "This map shows several locations around the mansion and in the surrounding area that appear to have historical significance. They could be related to the events and rituals that the mirror revealed."

Emily was going through some letters they had found by the mirror. "Some of these letters appear to be communications between members of the secret society and other influential individuals of the time. There are references to secret meetings and rituals that took place in different places."

Daniel, who had been reviewing historical documents about the resistance during World War II, looked up. "Based on what I found, some of the objects and documents that were hidden in the warehouse had a connection to the resistance, but they were also related to the dark events of the Whitmore family. It seems that there was a broader conspiracy at play."

The conversation centered on a figure mentioned in several letters: a prominent member of the secret society known as Charles Donovan. Donovan had been a key figure in the preservation and expansion of the dark covenant. The letters revealed that Donovan had maintained contact with several other members and had participated in numerous rituals.

"It appears that Charles Donovan played a crucial role in the conspiracy to keep the dark pact in place," Lisa commented. "We need to do more research on him and his role in the history of the Whitmore family."

The group decided to track down the story of Charles Donovan. The investigations led them to a number of historical records indicating that Donovan had been involved in several important events in recent history and that he had had a significant influence on the development of the dark pact.

A record revealed that Donovan had been a prominent member of a secret organization that had operated in the shadows during the war and had been associated with the old family diary. The connection between Donovan and the dark pact seemed deeper than they had imagined.

Lisa, Daniel, and Emily decided that they should investigate Donovan's legacy further. They found a number of documents in the historical archives that suggested that Donovan had carried out rituals in specific locations around the Whitmore mansion. These places included a number of old houses and buildings that were connected to the family's history.

The group began visiting these places, starting with an old farmhouse nearby that had been used as a meeting point for members of the secret society. The house was in ruins and had been abandoned, but historical documents indicated that it had been a key place for Donovan's rituals.

"This house seems to have been an important center of operations for Donovan," Daniel remarked, as they explored the crumbling rooms. "There could be evidence of the rituals he performed here."

While searching the house, Lisa discovered a series of esoteric symbols etched into the walls and floor. The symbols matched those they had seen in the Mirror of Truth and in the documents related to the dark covenant.

"These symbols are similar to the ones we saw in the mirror," Lisa said. "It seems that Donovan was performing rituals related to the dark covenant in this place."

Emily found a hidden compartment in the wall that contained a number of old documents and objects. Among these items were a number of letters and journals detailing Donovan's activities and his influence on the Whitmore family. The letters revealed that Donovan had been involved in a series of conspiracies to keep the dark pact active and expand his influence.

"The discovery of these documents provides a clearer view of how Donovan was trying to ensure the perpetuity of the pact," Emily said. "It appears that there was an elaborate plan to keep the pact in place and control the Whitmore family."

The group continued their research, visiting other locations related to Donovan's story and the dark pact. They found more evidence of rituals and conspiracies that had been going on for decades. Each discovery provided them with a deeper understanding of how the dark pact had influenced the history of the Whitmore family.

Finally, the group gathered enough information to chart a timeline of events related to the dark pact and Donovan's influence. They discovered that Donovan had been involved in a number of significant historical events, from the American Revolution to World War II, and that his influence had been a key factor in perpetuating the dark pact.

"We have a pretty complete view of Donovan's influence and the dark pact on the history of the Whitmore family," Lisa said, as they reviewed the timeline. "However, there are still unanswered questions about how the pact has remained active over time."

The group decided to conduct one last investigation into the Whitmore mansion to look for any additional evidence that might explain how the dark pact had been kept secret. They checked hidden areas and rooms that had not been previously explored.

During the search, they found a number of ancient documents and esoteric objects that were hidden in a secret room in the basement of the mansion. These documents provided details about the rituals that had been used to keep the covenant dark and ensure that its influence endured.

"These documents reveal how the pact has been kept active over time," Daniel said, as he reviewed the papers. "It appears that there have been a number of rituals and procedures that have been used to ensure the perpetuity of the covenant."

With the information obtained, Lisa, Daniel, and Emily were ready to face the ultimate challenge of completely neutralizing the dark pact's influence and securing the future of the Whitmore family. They knew they had unraveled a deep and complex conspiracy that had been afoot for generations, and they were determined to protect the family's legacy.

The group continued to work on their plan to ensure that the dark covenant was completely disabled. They knew their mission was coming to an end, but they also understood that the work they had done had been crucial to protecting the Whitmore family's future.

Chapter 31

The Whitmore mansion seemed enveloped in tense silence as Lisa, Daniel, and Emily prepared to perform the final ritual that they hoped would seal the dark pact's influence once and for all. Information gleaned from the Mirror of Truth and documents relating to Charles Donovan and the secret society had provided a deeper understanding of the history and nature of the pact, but now it was time to face the final challenge.

The mansion's office had been transformed into a center of operations for the ritual. Lisa, Daniel, and Emily had gathered all the necessary artifacts and documents, including the Mirror of Truth, esoteric symbols discovered in the old houses, and ancient texts about the dark covenant.

"Everything is ready for the ritual," Lisa said, as she reviewed the preparations in the office. "We have put together everything necessary to ensure that the dark pact is completely neutralized."

Daniel was reviewing the final details of the ritual. "The family diary provides detailed instructions on how to carry out the ritual. We must follow each step with precision to ensure that the covenant is effectively sealed."

Emily was going through the final documents they had found in the secret room in the basement. "We must also be prepared for any side effects or resistance that may arise during the ritual. The dark pact has been an important part of the Whitmore family's history, and there may be forces that try to interfere."

With everything in place, the group began the ritual following the instructions in the diary. They placed the Mirror of Truth in the center of the office and began to trace the esoteric symbols on the floor around the mirror. The symbols were arranged in a complex pattern that had to be carefully followed.

As the ritual progressed, the atmosphere in the mansion became denser and more charged. Candlelight and esoteric symbols created a mystical aura in the office, and the group worked with concentration and precision.

Lisa began to recite the words of the spell, as indicated in the diary. Lisa's voice echoed in the office as she recited the ancient words, and the Mirror of Truth began to glow with a dim light. The light intensified as the ritual progressed, and the mirror showed images of past events related to the dark covenant.

Daniel and Emily continued with the next stages of the ritual, adding ingredients and performing specific movements according to the instructions in the diary. As the ritual progressed, the office was filled with palpable energy, and the group felt a growing pressure in the air.

Suddenly, the atmosphere changed. The mirror began to show haunting visions of hooded figures and dark rituals. The images seemed to stand between the group and the success of the ritual, and a sense of resistance came over the office.

"There seems to be an active resistance," Emily said, as she looked at the visions in the mirror. "We must continue with the ritual and stay focused. The influence of the dark covenant may be trying to interfere."

Lisa stepped up the recitation of the spell, and Daniel and Emily redoubled their efforts to follow the ritual's instructions. The light from the mirror became more intense, and the images began to distort, showing scenes of resistance and internal struggle.

The office was filled with a magical glow as the ritual reached its climax. Lisa, Daniel, and Emily felt like the dark covenant energy was fading, but there was also a sense of exhaustion and tension. The pact's resistance seemed to be subsiding, but the group knew they needed to stay focused until the end.

Finally, the brightness of the Mirror of Truth reached its peak, and the visions began to fade. The light slowly faded, and the atmosphere in the office calmed down. The group had completed the ritual successfully.

Lisa slumped into a chair, exhausted but relieved. "We have managed to neutralize the influence of the dark pact. The ritual has been a success."

Daniel and Emily shared a look of relief as they reviewed the last details of the ritual. "The dark covenant has been sealed. The influence he's had on the Whitmore family should be over," Daniel said.

As the group recovered, they reflected on the impact of their mission and the effort they had put into solving the dark pact riddle. They knew that their work had not been in vain and that they had protected the future of the Whitmore family.

Lisa, Daniel, and Emily were ready to take on the next challenge. Although the dark pact had been neutralized, they knew that there were still questions to be answered and that the legacy of the Whitmore family had to be handled with care.

With the ritual completed and the dark pact sealed, the group prepared to close the final chapter of their investigation. The Whitmore mansion, now free from the influence of the pact, was preparing for a new beginning.

Chapter 32

Lisa, Daniel, and Emily were in the office of the Whitmore mansion, exhausted but relieved after having completed the ritual that neutralized the influence of the dark pact. However, a sense of unease lingered in the air. Despite the success of the ritual, they knew that there were still unresolved issues and that there could be unexpected consequences.

"Everything seems to be quiet now," Lisa said, as she looked at the office. "But there is something in the air that does not leave me calm. Maybe we should check the mansion again to make sure everything is in order."

Daniel and Emily nodded in agreement. The group decided to split up to inspect the mansion and verify that there was no residual influence left from the dark pact. Lisa made her way to the library, Daniel to the basement, and Emily to the outer areas of the mansion.

Lisa walked through the silent hallways, feeling a mixture of relief and apprehension. The library was in disarray after the ritual, with books and documents strewn across the floor. As she began to pick up and rearrange the papers, Lisa found an old trunk that she hadn't noticed before.

"This wasn't here before," Lisa thought, as she opened the trunk carefully. Inside he found a series of documents and objects that seemed to be related to the dark pact. One of the documents, however, caught his attention. It was a letter sealed with a family emblem, which had been hidden at the bottom of the trunk.

Lisa broke the seal and began to read the letter. The letter was written in elegant handwriting and detailed a contingency plan in case the dark pact was threatened. The letter spoke of a "hidden resource" that had been kept secret to ensure that the pact could be reactivated in case of emergency.

Meanwhile, in the basement, Daniel was going through the old documents and artifacts that had been discovered in the secret room. The basement was filled with dust and cobwebs, and the atmosphere was dense and charged. While going through a hidden compartment, he found an object that seemed to be related to the rituals of the dark covenant.

"This seems important," Daniel commented, examining an ancient spell book that had been hidden in a box. The book contained instructions on rituals that could be used to summon dark forces and keep the pact active. It was evident that the book had been kept for the purpose of reviving the covenant in case it was threatened.

In the outer areas of the mansion, Emily was surveying the gardens and surrounding grounds. Night was beginning to fall, and a light breeze was stirring the leaves of the trees. Emily would check the surroundings for any signs of suspicious activity.

While inspecting an old shed in the garden, he found a number of esoteric symbols etched into the walls and floor. The symbols were similar to those they had found in the lodge and office, and seemed to indicate that the place had been used for dark rituals.

Emily was about to examine further when she received a call from Lisa. "Emily, we found something troubling. It seems that there is a contingency plan to reactivate the dark pact. We must meet and discuss this."

The group met again in the office to share their findings. Lisa showed the letter she had found, and Daniel showed the spell book she had discovered in the basement. Emily explained the esoteric symbols she had found in the garden shed.

"It appears that the dark covenant had a strategy to stay active in case it was threatened," Lisa said, as she reviewed the letter. "These symbols in the shed and spellbook indicate that there could be more hidden artifacts and rituals that could be used to reactivate the covenant."

Daniel was worried. "If there is a chance that the dark pact can be reactivated, we must act quickly to ensure that everything is under control. The letter mentions a hidden resource that could be key in this process."

The group decided that they should locate the hidden resource mentioned in the letter and ensure that it could not be used to revive the pact. Lisa, Daniel, and Emily began searching for clues to the location of the hidden resource.

The letter stated that the resource was hidden in a location related to the history of the Whitmore family and the dark pact. After reviewing historical documents and maps, the group identified one possible location: an ancient underground crypt on the mansion's grounds.

"The hidden resource must be in the underground crypt," Lisa said. "We need to investigate that place and make sure it's fully secured."

The group made their way to the entrance to the crypt, which was hidden under a trapdoor in the garden. With a combination of effort and tools, they managed to open the trapdoor and descended into the crypt.

The crypt was a dark and damp place, full of cobwebs and dust. Lisa, Daniel, and Emily moved forward cautiously, lighting the way with flashlights. The crypt contained a series of chambers and niches, and the group began searching for the hidden resource mentioned in the letter.

After exploring several chambers, they found a hidden compartment in a stone wall. Inside the compartment was a wooden box sealed with a family emblem. The box was decorated with esoteric symbols that matched those they had found in the documents and in the garden shed.

Lisa carefully opened the box and found an ancient esoteric artifact that seemed to be the key to the hidden resource. The artifact was accompanied by a series of documents and rituals detailing how to use it to keep the dark pact active.

"This artifact is the hidden device mentioned in the letter," Lisa said, as she examined the contents of the box. "We must ensure that this device cannot be used to revive the pact."

The group decided that the artifact and documents should be destroyed to prevent any possibility that the dark pact could be reactivated. They carefully took the artifact outside the crypt and destroyed it in a safe place, following the instructions of the diary and documents related to the dark pact.

With the artifact destroyed and the hidden resource secured, the group was relieved. They knew that they had taken important steps to protect the future of the Whitmore family and ensure that the dark pact could not be reactivated.

"It's been a tough challenge, but we've managed to neutralize the imminent threat," Lisa said, as the group returned to the mansion. "We can now be sure that the dark pact is completely neutralized."

Daniel and Emily nodded, satisfied with the outcome of their mission. The group prepared to face the next step in their investigation and to close the final chapter of their story.

The Whitmore mansion, now free from the influence of the dark covenant and secured against any future threats, was ready for a fresh start. Lisa, Daniel, and Emily were determined to protect the Whitmore family's legacy and ensure that the dark past would never resurface.

Chapter 33

Calm seemed to have settled in the Whitmore mansion after the successful ritual. Lisa, Daniel, and Emily were in the office, going through the latest documents related to the dark pact and the artifacts they had discovered. However, a sense of unease still lingered. Despite having neutralized the influence of the pact, there was something that did not seem to quite fit.

"Now that we've secured the hidden resource, we should focus on any other details that may be related to the dark pact," Lisa said, as she reviewed the remaining documents. "There are still things I don't fully understand."

Emily was going through the spell book they had found in the basement. "This book contains rituals and spells that could have been used to keep the covenant active. There are some sections that appear to be encrypted or scrambled. Maybe we could try to figure them out."

Daniel was reviewing the letters and documents related to Charles Donovan. "The family diary also mentions that there were a number of hidden secrets that could only be revealed under certain circumstances. Maybe we should dig deeper to see if there's anything else we haven't discovered yet."

As the group continued to review the information, they began to notice patterns and connections they hadn't seen before. The documents and artifacts appeared to be interrelated in a way that suggested a more complex plan behind the dark pact.

Lisa noticed that there were a number of coordinates and symbols in the spellbook that could be related to the location of some additional artifact or a secret chamber. "These symbols and coordinates could be the key to finding something we haven't discovered yet. We must continue to investigate."

The group decided to follow the clues they had found in the documents and the spell book. The coordinates and symbols seemed to point to a specific location on the mansion grounds, beyond the crypt they had already explored.

They went to the location indicated by the coordinates, which was in a secluded area of the garden. There they found a series of stones and marks on the ground that matched the symbols in the spellbook. Apparently, there was a mechanism hidden in the ground that seemed to be linked to the location of a possible artifact.

After investigating the area, Lisa discovered an underground compartment hidden beneath the stones. The compartment contained a number of objects and documents that were related to the dark covenant and the history of the Whitmore family.

Among the objects found were a number of ancient scrolls that contained information about rituals and ceremonies that had not been previously documented. There was also an old medallion with a family emblem on it that seemed to have significant significance.

"This medallion could be key to understanding how the dark covenant has been maintained over time," Lisa said, as she examined the medallion. "It could have been used in rituals to ensure the perpetuity of the covenant."

Emily began to go through the ancient scrolls and discovered that they contained details about additional rituals and secrets that had been hidden for generations. "These scrolls reveal information about ceremonies and rituals that we did not know about. It seems that there was a secret network of rituals meant to keep the dark pact active."

Daniel, meanwhile, was reviewing documents that appeared to be instructions for the use of the medallion in specific rituals. "These documents indicate that the medallion had an important role in the performance of rituals. It may have been used to summon dark forces or to keep the pact active."

With the information obtained, the group realized that there was a wider network of rituals and secrets that had been used to secure the influence of the dark pact. The network included a series of ceremonies and objects that had been used to keep the pact active over time.

Lisa, Daniel, and Emily decided that they must unravel all the hidden secrets and ensure that no influence of the dark pact could persist. They began to work on the interpretation of the scrolls and on the decipherment of the rituals that had been revealed.

As they worked, the group noticed that documents and scrolls revealed details about a number of rituals that had been performed in different locations around the mansion. These rituals were designed to invoke dark forces and ensure the perpetuity of the covenant.

With the information obtained, the group decided to conduct a series of searches in the locations mentioned in the documents. They wanted to make sure that there were no more hidden artifacts or rituals that could be used to reactivate the dark pact.

Searches of the aforementioned locations revealed a number of hidden chambers and esoteric objects that were linked to covenant rituals. The group found evidence that the network of rituals and objects was more widespread than they had imagined.

As they explored these locations, the group began to understand the magnitude of the dark pact's influence and the complexity of the secret network that had been created to keep it active. It was evident that the pact had had a significant impact on the history of the Whitmore family and on the secret society that had perpetuated it.

Finally, with all secrets revealed and artifacts secured, the group was relieved to learn that they had done everything they could to protect the Whitmore family's future. They had neutralized the dark covenant's influence and dismantled the web of rituals and secrets that had sustained it for generations.

The Whitmore mansion, now free from the influence of the dark covenant and any future threats, was ready for a fresh start. Lisa, Daniel, and Emily were determined to close this chapter of history and ensure that the Whitmore family's legacy was handled with care and responsibility.

Chapter 34

The calm in the Whitmore mansion was deceptive. Lisa, Daniel, and Emily had taken a breather after their recent discoveries, but a lingering sense that something else might be at play kept everyone on their toes. Although the dark pact had been neutralized and the hidden artifacts secured, Lisa still felt an uneasiness that she could not fully comprehend.

One night, while going through the documents and ancient scrolls, Lisa discovered an old diary that had been overlooked. The diary was written in elegant calligraphy and contained notes that seemed to be more personal than the other documents they had found.

"This is new," Lisa said, as she opened the journal and began to read the entries. The diary appeared to belong to one of the Whitmore family's ancestors, and it contained intimate details about that family member's life and personal struggles.

The entries revealed a series of events and decisions that appeared to be linked to the dark pact. The author of the diary had mentioned several times a "family secret" that had been jealously guarded and that was related to a series of dark events that had affected the Whitmore family over the years.

Lisa shared her findings with Daniel and Emily, and the group decided it was crucial to delve deeper into the personal history of the Whitmore family's ancestors. "There could be details in this journal that explain some of the things that we don't fully understand," Lisa said.

Daniel and Emily began researching the historical context and circumstances surrounding the diary entries. The investigation revealed that the author of the diary had been a key member of the secret society linked to the dark pact and that he had made important decisions to ensure his influence.

Meanwhile, Lisa continued to read the diary and found an entry that spoke of a series of events that occurred in the mansion that seemed to be linked to paranormal phenomena. The author mentioned that he had witnessed visions and felt an unsettling presence in the mansion, suggesting that the influence of the dark covenant may have had a more profound impact than initially believed.

With the information obtained from the diary, the group decided to conduct a more thorough investigation into the mansion, looking for clues about the visions and the disturbing presence that had been mentioned in the entries. Lisa, Daniel, and Emily headed to the less-explored areas of the mansion, checking out nooks and crannies and rooms that hadn't been inspected in detail before.

In the basement of the mansion, they found an old closet hidden behind a false wall. Inside the closet were a number of documents and objects that were linked to rituals and paranormal events. They also found an old portrait of one of the ancestors of the Whitmore family, the same one who had written the diary.

"The portrait seems to be related to the visions I mentioned in the diary," Lisa said, as she examined the portrait. "There could be some connection between this person and the paranormal phenomena we are investigating."

Daniel was going through the documents and found references to a number of rituals that had been carried out at the mansion to attempt to control or communicate with paranormal entities. "These documents suggest that there were attempts to manipulate paranormal forces that could have been part of the dark pact. The disturbing presence mentioned in the diary could be a manifestation of these forces."

Emily went through the objects found in the closet and discovered a number of artifacts that seemed to be linked to paranormal rituals. "These artifacts could have been used in rituals to summon or control entities. We may need to make sure that these objects are neutralized as well."

The group decided that they should carry out a series of cleansing and protection rituals to ensure that any residual influence of the paranormal entities was removed. They used the knowledge acquired from the diary and documents to perform rituals that sought to neutralize any residual influence and protect the mansion from future manifestations.

During the rituals, the group experienced a series of paranormal phenomena that confirmed the presence of entities in the mansion. Flickering lights, unexplained noises, and a feeling of intense cold filled the air, but with each step they took in the ritual, it seemed that the influence of the entities was fading.

Finally, after performing the rituals and securing the mansion, the group felt that the atmosphere in the mansion had stabilized. The sense of unease they had felt before seemed to have disappeared, and the mansion finally felt free of dark and paranormal influences.

"We seem to have managed the residual influence effectively," Lisa said, as the group gathered in the office. "The mansion should be free of any dark or paranormal influences now."

Daniel and Emily agreed that the research and additional rituals had been crucial to ensuring the safety and well-being of the mansion. With the feeling that the dark past had been dealt with in a comprehensive manner, the group prepared to close this chapter and begin to think about the future.

The Whitmore mansion, once again, was ready for a fresh start. Lisa, Daniel, and Emily were relieved to learn that they had gone to great lengths to ensure that the Whitmore family's legacy was handled with care and responsibility.

Chapter 35

The atmosphere in the Whitmore mansion had changed significantly since paranormal influences and the dark pact had been handled. However, a sense of incompleteness still lingered between Lisa, Daniel, and Emily. Despite the efforts made, they felt that there were still aspects of the mystery that needed to be solved before they could finally close the chapter in the Whitmore family's history.

One afternoon, while going through the remaining documents in the office, Lisa found a letter that appeared to have been written by one of the most recent members of the Whitmore family. The letter was dated the 1970s and appeared to be a personal will that had been carefully kept.

"This is interesting," Lisa commented, showing the letter to Daniel and Emily. "It seems to be a will or a personal letter that we had not found before. Maybe you can give us more information about the Whitmore family and their secrets."

Emily examined the letter and noticed that it spoke of a number of personal and family events, as well as a "deep secret" that needed to be revealed at the right time. The letter mentioned that the secret was related to a series of objects and documents that had been hidden in a specific place in the mansion.

"It could be that there are more secrets hidden in the mansion," Emily said, as she read the letter. "The mention of a 'deep secret' suggests that there may be something else we haven't discovered yet."

Daniel reviewed the document and began to look for clues as to the location of the secret mentioned in the letter. "The letter mentions a specific place in the mansion where the objects related to the secret were kept. We must look in that area."

The letter stated that the secret was hidden in a hidden compartment in the attic of the mansion, a place they had not previously inspected in detail. The group decided to investigate the attic with the aim of finding the compartment and unraveling the secret.

They went up to the attic, which was filled with antique objects, dust-covered furniture, and stacked boxes. The place had an air of abandonment, but also of history, and the group began to carefully check the area for any clues.

While going through the boxes and furniture, Lisa found a wall that appeared to have a hidden panel. "This doesn't seem to be aligned with the rest of the structure. There may be something hidden here."

Carefully, Lisa and Daniel began clearing the area and examining the panel. After a few moments of work, they managed to open the panel and discovered a hidden compartment behind it. Inside the compartment were a number of documents, antique objects and a wooden box with a family emblem.

"It looks like we've found what we were looking for," Lisa said, as she opened the box. Inside were several old documents, letters, and a number of objects that seemed to have special meaning to the Whitmore family.

The documents included a number of letters and records detailing important events in the Whitmore family's history, as well as a number of esoteric objects that were related to dark covenant rituals and ceremonies. Among the objects found was an ancient book that contained details about the history and secrets of the Whitmore family.

Emily reviewed the book and found that it contained information about a number of dark events that had affected the family over the years. The book also revealed details about the founding of the dark covenant and how it had influenced the family's history.

"This book reveals important details about the history of the family and the dark covenant," Emily said, as she read the pages. "There seems to be a deep connection between personal events and family secrets."

Daniel found a series of letters that were addressed to different members of the Whitmore family. The letters contained information about the decisions that had been made to protect the family's secrets and about how dark events had been handled over time.

"The correspondence reveals that there were a number of decisions and strategies used to keep the family's secrets and manage dark influences," Daniel said. "It appears that there was a conscious effort on the part of the family to protect these secrets and make sure they were not revealed."

With the information gleaned from the documents and objects, the group began to understand the magnitude of the secrets that had been kept by the Whitmore family. The documents revealed a complex web of rituals, decisions, and events that had influenced the family's history and the secret society that had perpetuated the dark pact.

Lisa, Daniel, and Emily realized that despite having neutralized the dark covenant's influence and secured the mansion, it was crucial to fully understand the secrets revealed in order to handle the Whitmore family's legacy properly.

"Now that we have found these secrets, we must ensure that the family's history and legacy are handled with care," Lisa said. "We must record and preserve this information so that the Whitmore family's future can be built on a solid foundation."

The group decided that it was important to record all the information obtained and to ensure that the family's secrets were understood and respected. They began working on documentation and creating a detailed archive that would preserve the history and secrets of the Whitmore family.

As they worked, Lisa, Daniel, and Emily reflected on the impact they had had on the family's history and on the Whitmore mansion. They knew they had taken important steps to protect the legacy and ensure that the dark covenant could not resurface.

The Whitmore mansion, now full of history and secrets revealed, was ready for a new beginning. Lisa, Daniel, and Emily were satisfied with the work they had done and the deep understanding they had gained about the family's dark past.

With the knowledge gained and secrets revealed, the group was ready to close this chapter and prepare for the future, knowing that they had handled the Whitmore family's legacy with care and responsibility.

Chapter 36

The Whitmore mansion had been transformed into a place of calm and reflection following the recent discovery of hidden family secrets and the neutralization of the dark pact's influence. Lisa, Daniel, and Emily had spent a lot of time reviewing and recording all the information they had found, and they were ready to face the last part of their mission: to make sure that the Whitmore family's legacy was properly preserved and the dark past completely closed.

It was a sunny afternoon when the group gathered in the mansion's library to discuss their next steps. The space was filled with ancient books, documents, and esoteric objects that had been recovered during his research. The atmosphere was charged with a sense of accomplishment, but also a slight unease, as they knew that there were still details to be worked out.

"Now that we've figured out everything we could about the family's past and the dark pact, we need to decide how to handle the information and what to do with the objects and documents we've found," Lisa said, looking at her companions. "We must make sure that none of this falls into the wrong hands."

Daniel, who had been reviewing the old letters and documents, added: "The correspondence suggests that the Whitmore family had taken precautions to protect their secrets, and I think we should follow that tradition. Information should be stored securely and accessible only to those who need to know it."

Emily was examining the esoteric objects and artifacts recovered. "We must also consider what to do with artifacts linked to the dark covenant and rituals. We cannot allow these items to be used to reactivate the covenant or to summon dark forces again."

Lisa nodded, understanding the importance of her observations. "We can create a detailed file with all the information we have found and make sure that dangerous objects are stored in a safe place. We should also consider consulting with experts in history and esotericism to make sure we are handling everything correctly."

Determined to close this chapter of history properly, the group began to work on the organization and storage of information. They were in charge of sorting through documents, recording relevant information, and making sure everything was properly filed.

Lisa, while going through the ancient ritual book, found a section that appeared to have been written in a coded language. "This book has sections that we have not fully deciphered. Perhaps it is crucial to ensure that no details are left unresolved."

With the help of Daniel and Emily, they began to decipher the encrypted section of the book. They discovered that it contained additional information about rituals and ceremonies that had been used to protect the dark covenant and ensure its perpetuity. The information was complex, but by deciphering it, they were able to better understand the extent of the rituals and methods used to maintain the covenant.

While they were working on the documents and deciphered information, Lisa received an unexpected call from her mentor, Dr. Richard Hughes. "Lisa, I've been reviewing the information you've sent me and I think it's crucial that we review some final details before we close this chapter. There are aspects of the dark pact and the history of the Whitmore family that could use more clarification."

Lisa, worried about the call, brought Daniel and Emily together to discuss next steps. "Dr. Hughes wants to review some final details with us. We must prepare for any new information that may arise."

Dr. Hughes arrived at the mansion and met the group in the library. They began to go through the information and documents that had been found, discussing the details and clarifying any questions that arose.

During the review, Dr. Hughes made an important observation. "There is a detail in the documents that suggests the existence of a final ritual or ceremony that could have been used to cement the dark covenant. This ritual could have been designed to ensure that the covenant could not be easily dismantled."

The group, surprised by the observation, decided to investigate further the detail mentioned by Dr. Hughes. They re-examined the documents and found a reference to a final ritual that had been mentioned in one of the letters and in the ritual book.

"It seems that the final ritual was designed to ensure the permanence of the covenant and to protect the family's secrets," Lisa said. "We must ensure that this ritual has not been completed or used in a way that may affect the influence of the covenant."

With the new information, the group conducted a thorough search of the mansion and the surrounding area to ensure that there were no indications that the final ritual had been performed. Fortunately, they found no evidence that the ritual had been carried out.

With the certainty that the dark pact had been neutralized and that the Whitmore family's secrets had been properly handled, the group was relieved. The mansion was ready for a fresh start, free of dark influences and with a preserved legacy.

Lisa, Daniel, and Emily said goodbye to Dr. Hughes, thanking him for his help and guidance throughout the process. They knew they had gone to great lengths to ensure that the Whitmore family's story was handled with care and responsibility.

The Whitmore mansion, now full of history and secrets revealed, was prepared for a bright future. Lisa, Daniel, and Emily were satisfied with the work done and were ready to close this chapter, knowing that they had properly protected and preserved the Whitmore family's legacy.

Chapter 37: New Horizons

After weeks of intense research and exhaustive work at the Whitmore mansion, Lisa, Daniel, and Emily had finally concluded their mission. The history of the Whitmore family had been unraveled, dark secrets had been neutralized, and the family's legacy was ready to be preserved. The mansion, now free of paranormal influences, was preparing for a new chapter.

The sun shone on the mansion, giving it an air of renewal and hope. Lisa, as she looked out over the sprawling gardens from one of the windows in the main living room, reflected on the long journey they had travelled. The mansion had been the scene of dark secrets, but now it was transforming into a place of peace and clarity.

Daniel and Emily were busy organizing the final paperwork and preparing the mansion for its transition into a new era. They had decided that the mansion would become a center of study and historical preservation, where the events and secrets of the Whitmore family could be researched and understood in a broader context.

"The file is almost ready," Daniel said, as he reviewed the documents in the office. "We've done a great job preserving history and ensuring that secrets are handled properly."

Emily was organizing the esoteric objects in a special room intended for safe storage. "Making sure these devices are protected and kept in a safe place is critical. We cannot allow them to fall into the wrong hands."

Lisa joined them in the office, a determined expression on her face. "I think we're ready to take the next step. The mansion should not only be a place of study, but also a symbol of renewal and learning. We must ensure that the legacy of the Whitmore family serves as a warning and a lesson for future generations."

As the group discussed plans for the future of the mansion, they received an unexpected visitor. It was a local historian, Dr. Samuel Carter, who had heard about the recent discoveries and was interested in learning more about the history of the Whitmore family.

"Dr. Carter has shown a great interest in the findings and in the history of the mansion," Lisa said, as she greeted the historian in the main hall. "I think he could be a great ally in our mission to preserve and share the family's legacy."

Dr. Carter, a middle-aged man with an intellectual appearance and an inquisitive attitude, greeted Lisa, Daniel, and Emily enthusiastically. "I have closely followed recent discoveries and am impressed by the work they have done. The history of the Whitmore family is fascinating, and I believe their work has the potential to contribute significantly to the study of local history and the understanding of paranormal phenomena."

Lisa and her team shared with Dr. Carter the details of their findings and plans for the future of the mansion. The historian was excited for the opportunity to collaborate and offer his expertise to ensure that the Whitmore family's story was properly understood and shared.

"I would love to collaborate on creating an exhibit about the Whitmore family and the events that have taken place here," Dr. Carter said. "We could work together to create a research center that attracts scholars and curious people alike, and preserves history for future generations."

The group eagerly accepted Dr. Carter's offer and began working on the details to establish the research center in the mansion. The project included creating interactive exhibits, organizing conferences, and publishing research on the history of the Whitmore family and paranormal events.

As they worked on preparing the mansion for their new role, Lisa, Daniel, and Emily reflected on the impact of their work. They had faced and overcome numerous challenges, unraveling dark secrets and ensuring that the Whitmore family's legacy was preserved.

"This is just the beginning," Lisa said, as she watched the preparations underway. "The research center will be a place where important lessons can be learned about history, the power of secrets and the importance of facing the past with courage."

The team worked tirelessly to prepare the mansion for its opening as a research center. They created detailed exhibits, organized lectures, and established a comprehensive archive of the Whitmore family's history and paranormal events.

Finally, the day of the inauguration of the research center arrived. The Whitmore mansion was filled with scholars, researchers, and curious onlookers who were eager to learn the history and secrets that had been revealed. Lisa, Daniel, and Emily were satisfied to see that their work had led to a new chapter in the mansion's history.

During the inauguration, Dr. Carter gave a speech in which he highlighted the importance of the work carried out and the relevance of the research center. "The Whitmore mansion is not only a testament to the past, but also a symbol of the search for truth and understanding. This center will be a place where history will be preserved and the events that have taken place here will be learned."

Lisa, observing the inauguration, felt a deep satisfaction. They had faced numerous challenges and had managed to transform a place of darkness into a beacon of knowledge and reflection. The Whitmore mansion, now free of dark influences, was prepared for a future full of possibilities and opportunities.

With the research center underway and the Whitmore family's history finally exposed, Lisa, Daniel, and Emily were ready to move on. They knew that their work had made a difference and that the legacy of the Whitmore family would live on in the minds and hearts of those who came to learn from their history.

Chapter 38

The Whitmore mansion, now immersed in relative calm, was preparing to face its last phase of transformation. Lisa, Daniel, and Emily were in the main office, a space that had been central to solving the dark mysteries surrounding the Whitmore family. The air was charged with a sense of closure and anticipation, as they were about to complete the last act of their mission.

Lisa reviewed the latest notes and documents that had been meticulously classified and filed. The work had been arduous, but the efforts had been worth it. The sun filtered through the windows of the office, bathing the space in a warm light that contrasted with the atmosphere of tension that had dominated the mansion for so long.

"Everything is almost ready for the grand opening," Lisa commented, as she organized the final documents. "The archive is complete and we have prepared everything for the inauguration of the research center."

Daniel was reviewing the logistical details of the inauguration. "I have confirmed the schedules with the suppliers and the security team. Everything is in order to receive guests and present the mansion as a center of historical research."

Emily, meanwhile, was finalizing preparations for the exhibition to be held at the center. "The exhibits are ready and the information panels are in place. I'm reviewing the final details to make sure the information is clear and accessible."

The group took a moment to reflect on the work they had done. The mansion, which had once been a place of dark secrets and betrayals, was about to become a place of knowledge and learning. The opening of the research center would be the perfect closure to their mission, and the beginning of a new era for the Whitmore family.

Suddenly, the door to the office opened and Dr. Samuel Carter, the local historian who had been collaborating with them, entered. He brought with him an expression of concern. "Lisa, Daniel, Emily, I need to talk to you. Something has happened."

Lisa looked up, noticing the seriousness on Dr. Carter's face. "What happened?"

"I received a tip that someone has been attempting to gain access to the mansion without permission," Dr. Carter explained. "We don't know if it's just a curiosity or if someone is trying to interfere with the work we've done."

Lisa's heart raced. "Do you have any idea who might be behind this?"

"I'm not sure, but I think we need to take precautions," Dr. Carter replied. "It could be someone with unclear intentions about the Whitmore family's secrets or someone who just wants to take advantage of the story for their own gain."

Lisa and Daniel looked at each other, recognizing the need to act quickly. "We are going to investigate and make sure that everything is in order before the inauguration. We cannot allow anything to interfere with the work we have done."

Together, the group began to check the areas of the mansion to make sure everything was safe. Dr. Carter was in charge of reviewing the security cameras and alarm systems to verify that everything was working properly.

While checking the area, they found a window in the basement that appeared to have been forced. Lisa, flashlight in hand, scanned the basement and discovered signs of a recent unauthorized entry. Although it didn't look like anything had been stolen, the intrusion indicated that someone had been looking for something specific.

"This is disturbing," Lisa said, as she surveyed the area. "We must ensure that the entire mansion is properly protected."

Daniel and Emily were in charge of reinforcing security measures and checking all possible entrances and exits. They ensured that alarm systems were working and that all windows and doors were closed and locked.

With security measures in place, the group met to discuss their next steps. "We don't know who is behind this, but we must be prepared for any eventuality," Daniel said. "The inauguration cannot be postponed, and we must make sure that everything is ready for the event."

Opening day arrived, and the Whitmore mansion was ready to receive guests. The research center had been transformed into a modern and welcoming space, with exhibits detailing the history of the Whitmore family and the paranormal events that had taken place. The inauguration was a success, with academics, researchers and curious onlookers who came to learn about the family's legacy.

Throughout the event, Lisa, Daniel, and Emily made sure everything went smoothly, attending to visitors and answering questions. Dr. Carter gave a lecture on the history of the Whitmore family and the importance of the research center.

The opening went off without major incidents, and the group was relieved to see that their work had led to a new chapter in the mansion's history. The research center was now operational, and the Whitmore mansion was poised for a future of learning and reflection.

With the opening complete and the research center underway, Lisa, Daniel, and Emily were satisfied with the work done. They had faced challenges and overcome obstacles, and the Whitmore mansion was ready to welcome those who wished to know their history and learn from it.

The sense of accomplishment and closure grew stronger as the group reflected on their mission. They knew they had managed to transform a place of dark secrets into a beacon of knowledge and hope, and they were ready to move on, knowing that their work had made a significant difference.

Chapter 39

The Whitmore Mansion, now operational as a research center, was still in a state of vibrant activity. Scholars and experts came from far and wide, eager to examine the documents and artifacts that had been carefully preserved and presented. Lisa, Daniel, and Emily were busier than ever, organizing tours, answering questions, and managing the steady stream of visitors interested in the history of the Whitmore family.

The atmosphere in the mansion was one of constant enthusiasm, but also of latent tension. The recent intrusion they had experienced had left a sense of unease in the air, and although they had tightened security measures, the fear that something unexpected might happen was still present.

One afternoon, while Lisa was going through the file to prepare a presentation on the Whitmore family's findings, she received an urgent message from Daniel. "Lisa, you need to come to the basement. We found something we didn't expect."

The tone of the call was grave, and Lisa hurried downstairs to the basement. Daniel and Emily were already there, examining a small compartment hidden behind a wall. The box they had found was dusty and covered with cobwebs, and its appearance was of obvious antiquity.

"What have you found?" asked Lisa, as she approached.

Daniel turned to her, with a worried expression. "We found this hidden compartment. Inside it was a box that seemed to be meant to be kept secret. We don't know what's in it, but it seems to be important."

Emily, wearing gloves, was trying to open the box carefully. "It doesn't look like it's been touched in a long time. Let's see what's inside."

After a few minutes of work, they managed to open the box. Inside, they found several old documents, as well as a small leather journal that appeared to be in good condition despite its age.

Lisa picked up the journal with trembling hands and began to flip through it. The writing was elegant and clearly legible. As he read the first few pages, his face hardened. "This diary appears to have been written by one of the original members of the Whitmore family. It speaks of secrets and pacts that had never been revealed."

Daniel and Emily came over to read with her. The documents included references to dark rituals and mentions of a mysterious figure who appeared to have played a central role in the events that had occurred at the mansion.

"This diary mentions someone called The Custodian," Lisa said, as she read aloud. "It seems that he was a secret member of the family tasked with maintaining the dark pact and protecting the deepest secrets. We have no prior information about this individual."

Emily frowned. "If El Custodio was a key figure in keeping the pact, there may still be people who remember him or even remain loyal to his cause. This could be dangerous."

Lisa nodded. "Yes, and the fact that they hid these documents indicates that they might have tried to hide something important. We must be careful and make sure that this information does not fall into the wrong hands."

While they were discussing the find, Dr. Samuel Carter arrived at the basement, alerted by the activity. "What's going on here?"

Lisa showed him the diary and the documents. "We found this in a hidden compartment. It seems that The Custodian had a crucial role in the history of the Whitmore family and the secrets we've been trying to understand."

Dr. Carter examined the documents and the journal with interest. "This is fascinating. If The Custodian was involved in maintaining the dark pact, we need to investigate further to understand his role and ensure there are no residual influences."

The group decided that it was essential to investigate further into El Custodio and its possible influence on current events. Lisa, Daniel, Emily, and Dr. Carter began mapping out a plan to unravel more details about this mysterious figure and its impact on the Whitmore family.

One of the first things they did was to go through all the old documents and records related to the Whitmore family. They looked for any mention of El Custodio or related figures that could provide more information.

As they worked on the investigation, Lisa began to notice patterns in the diary's writing that seemed to indicate that The Custodian had been in contact with outside individuals, perhaps even other secret organizations. The newspaper also mentioned a specific location, an ancient monastery on the outskirts of the city, which appeared to have been a site of secret meetings.

"We must investigate this monastery," Lisa suggested. "It could be a key place to understand the role of El Custodio and what's really at stake."

The group decided that it was necessary to visit the monastery to explore the possibility of finding more clues. They prepared for the trip, making sure to bring with them all the necessary equipment to investigate and document their findings.

The monastery, located in a remote area, was in a state of neglect and decaying over time. As the group approached the building, the atmosphere became more somber and ominous. Lisa, Daniel, Emily, and Dr. Carter felt a chill run down their spines, knowing they were about to enter a place steeped in history and mystery.

Once inside the monastery, they began to explore the facilities. The place was littered with dust and cobwebs, but the group moved forward carefully, looking for any clues that might be related to The Custodian and his influence.

While exploring, they found a hidden room in the basement of the monastery. Inside the room, there were ancient manuscripts and artifacts that appeared to be related to dark rituals and ceremonies. They also found a small altar with strange symbols and a series of documents that mentioned El Custodio.

"This is what we were looking for," Lisa said, as she reviewed the documents. "It appears that The Custodian had a central role in performing rituals and ceremonies that kept the pact dark."

The group spent several hours in the monastery, examining the finds and documenting everything they found. They knew they had uncovered crucial information, but they were also aware that their investigation was far from over.

With the mission at the monastery completed, they returned to Whitmore Manor, intending to analyze the new documents and artifacts they had found. They were determined to fully understand the role of The Custodian and to ensure that any residual influence of the dark covenant was completely eradicated.

As the group delved deeper into the analysis of their findings, they understood that their mission was taking an unexpected turn. Although they had solved many of the mysteries, the echo of the past still echoed through the walls of the mansion and into the darkest corners of the Whitmore family's history.

Chapter 40

The atmosphere in the Whitmore mansion was charged with expectation. Lisa, Daniel, Emily, and Dr. Carter had gathered in the office to examine the new documents and artifacts found in the monastery. The find had revealed a number of disturbing connections to The Custodian, a central figure in the Whitmore family's dark secrets.

Lisa sat down at a table filled with ancient documents and manuscripts, while Daniel and Emily organized the artifacts found in the monastery. Dr. Carter was reviewing papers that contained cryptic symbols and texts related to dark rituals.

"It seems that we have found solid evidence that The Custodian was not only involved in the Whitmore family, but also had connections to other secret groups," Lisa commented, reviewing a manuscript that spoke of alliances between different esoteric organizations. "These documents suggest that El Custodio operated as an intermediary between various groups that shared an interest in maintaining and expanding the dark pact."

Daniel, examining an ancient scroll, nodded. "We also found references to a final ritual, which apparently was going to take place in a specific place, probably the same monastery we have visited. This ritual seems to be the climax of the series of dark pacts."

Emily, who was reviewing a ritual book, added: "There are detailed descriptions of the procedures of the ritual and how it was to be carried out. However, some passages are encrypted or scrambled, which could indicate that only certain individuals had full access to this information."

Dr. Carter, his face grave, rose and walked over to the table. "We must consider that El Custodio may have had followers or allies who might still be interested in the secrets of the pact. Our mission does not end here. We need to find out as much as we can about the ritual and potential followers to make sure there isn't a residual threat."

Lisa nodded, knowing that the group was at a critical point in their investigation. "We are going to work on deciphering the encrypted texts and looking for any clue about the location of El Custodio's followers. We must also prepare a strategy to protect the mansion and the research center from any possible interference attempts."

The team began working on the encoded texts, using analysis tools and cryptography techniques to decipher the information. As they progressed, they discovered that the final ritual was aimed at consolidating the power of the dark covenant and ensuring its perpetuity. The documents indicated that the ritual required a number of specific objects and the involvement of key individuals.

One of the nights, while the group was immersed in the analysis, Emily received an urgent phone call. The call was from a contact he had in the local police, who informed him that there had been an attempted robbery at the mansion. Although no important items had been taken, the incident was troubling.

"This is not a coincidence," Lisa said, after hearing the report. "Someone is trying to gain access to the mansion to get information about the secrets we've been handling."

Dr. Carter was worried. "We must step up security measures and make sure there are no gaps in the protection of the mansion. It is also critical that we keep information about the ritual and The Custodian as confidential as possible."

The group was in charge of reinforcing the security of the mansion and establishing additional measures to prevent future intrusion attempts. In the meantime, they continued to work on deciphering the texts and discovering more details about the ritual.

One morning, Daniel found an important clue in one of the decrypted documents. "There is a mention of a consecration ceremony that seems to be the final phase of the ritual. This ceremony would take place in a place of great significance to the followers of The Custodian, possibly a secret meeting place."

Lisa and Dr. Carter discussed the possible location of this location and concluded that it could be related to an old property linked to the Whitmore family. "We must investigate this place and verify if there is any connection to the final ritual," Lisa said. "We may find out more about El Custodio's followers and their intentions."

The group prepared to investigate the ancient property, which was located on the outskirts of the city. They made sure to bring all the necessary equipment for the investigation and took precautions to protect themselves in case they encountered resistance.

Upon arriving at the property, they found a dilapidated building that appeared to have been uninhabited for decades. The structure was in disrepair, with fallen walls and broken windows, but the group was determined to explore every corner.

While investigating the interior, they found esoteric symbols and markings on the walls indicating that the place had been used for dark rituals. They also discovered a number of documents hidden in an underground room, which appeared to be related to the consecration ceremony mentioned in the texts.

Lisa, when reviewing the documents, found a list of names and addresses that could be linked to the followers of El Custodio. "These names and addresses could be key to locating individuals who might still be involved in dark rituals," he said.

With the new information in hand, the group returned to the mansion to plan their next steps. They knew that the confrontation with the followers of El Custodio could be imminent and that they had to be prepared for any eventuality.

"We're going to work on locating these individuals and making sure that there's no threat to the security of the mansion and the research facility," Lisa said. "Our goal is to end any residual influence of the dark covenant and ensure that the Whitmore family's legacy serves as a cautionary lesson."

With renewed determination, the group prepared to face the challenges that lay ahead. They knew that the final solution to the Whitmore family's mysteries was within reach, and they were ready to uncover the full truth and ensure a future free from dark influences.

Chapter 41

The Whitmore mansion was in a quiet agitation. Recent investigation into the former property had revealed names and addresses that indicated the possible existence of active followers of El Custodio. Lisa, Daniel, Emily, and Dr. Carter were in an intense phase of preparation, ready to face whatever might come next. The threat of a possible confrontation with the followers of El Custodio felt imminent.

The group had gathered in the office to review the final details before taking action. The documents found on the ancient property had been analyzed and now focused on identifying the individuals mentioned in the texts.

"The addresses we found are spread out in different locations in and around the city," Lisa said, pointing to a map spread out on the table. "We must prioritize our actions to investigate these individuals and ensure that there is no plan in place to carry out the final ritual."

Emily, who was reviewing the list of names, added: "Some of these names seem to be linked to local organisations with a history of esoteric activities. They may already be in contact with other followers or even secretly preparing something."

Dr. Carter, who had been in contact with the local authorities, got up and walked over to the table. "I have spoken to some colleagues in the police. They are ready to assist us in the investigation and surveillance of places that we consider suspicious. We need to coordinate our efforts to ensure that all potential risk points are covered."

Daniel nodded. "We should split up to investigate the locations mentioned on the list. Emily and I can go to the addresses that seem most urgent, while Lisa and Dr. Carter can review the other locations and coordinate with law enforcement."

The group agreed on the plan of action and prepared to leave. The tension was palpable as each headed to their destination, aware that they might be about to unravel the final truth about The Custodian and the Dark Pact.

Lisa and Dr. Carter made their way to an old mansion on the outskirts of town, which was linked to one of the names on the list. The mansion was in a similar state of disrepair to the property they had previously investigated, but there seemed to be signs that someone had been occupying it recently.

While inspecting the place, Lisa found a number of documents and artifacts that were hidden in a secret compartment in the library. The documents contained information about the final ritual, including specific details about the steps needed to complete it.

"It seems that we have found a copy of the ritual proceedings," Lisa said, as she examined the papers. "This confirms that this place was being used to prepare the final ritual. We must take these documents to the police and make sure that the mansion is secured."

Meanwhile, Emily and Daniel arrived at an address that appeared to be a house in the suburbs, belonging to one of the names on the list. When investigating the property, they found a series of ritual objects and documents that indicated that the place was also linked to the followers of El Custodio.

"This house seems to be a gathering place for fans," Emily said. "We found clear evidence that they were preparing for something. We must inform Lisa and Dr. Carter immediately."

The group met again at the Whitmore mansion to review the findings and plan their next steps. With the information they had gathered, it was evident that the followers of El Custodio were in the process of carrying out the final ritual.

"We must act quickly," Lisa said. "Now that we have evidence that followers are preparing the ritual, we must prevent any attempt to complete it. The police must intervene and ensure that there is no activity in the identified places."

Dr. Carter, who had coordinated with authorities, reported that they were ready to conduct raids on properties linked to the followers. "The police have prepared teams to intervene in the places we have identified. Our goal is to stop any attempts to complete the ritual and ensure that everyone involved is taken into custody."

The group made their way to the properties with police, closely observing the actions to ensure that appropriate action was taken. Tension was high as the operations were underway, but the effort was worth it when the raids confirmed that followers were attempting to perform the final ritual.

With the followers arrested and the ritual stopped, the group returned to the Whitmore mansion. The sense of relief was palpable, but there was also a sense of reflection on the work they had done.

"I think we've managed to secure the mansion and the research center from any residual influence," Lisa said, as she looked at the now-quiet office. "The dark pact and the secrets of the Whitmore family have finally been confronted and dismantled."

Dr. Carter nodded. "Our research has uncovered the truth and allowed the research center to serve as a place of knowledge and learning. The history of the Whitmore family is complete, and the dark influence has been eradicated."

Emily and Daniel also expressed their satisfaction with the work done. "We have managed to transform a legacy of dark secrets into a center of truth and understanding," Emily said. "Our work has been hard, but it was worth it."

With the last chapter of the Whitmore family's history written, Lisa, Daniel, Emily, and Dr. Carter prepared to move forward into a future free from the shadows of the past. The Whitmore Mansion, now a beacon of knowledge, was ready to welcome those who sought to learn and understand the history of a family that had faced its own demons and emerged into the light.

Chapter 42

The Whitmore Mansion, renovated and transformed into a center of historical research, now stood as a symbol of knowledge and redemption. After intense investigations and confrontations, Lisa, Daniel, Emily, and Dr. Carter were at the height of their mission, watching as the place became a space for study and education.

The renovated mansion housed a series of exhibitions and laboratories dedicated to the history of the Whitmore family and the analysis of the findings obtained during the investigation. The sections devoted to the family's dark legacy had become areas of reflection and warning, with informational panels detailing past events and lessons learned.

Lisa, watching the preparations for the research center's grand opening, felt a mixture of pride and relief. Their work, along with the team's effort, had succeeded in transforming a dark legacy into a valuable resource for the community.

Daniel was overseeing the installation of a new exhibit in the main wing. The exhibit included a collection of artifacts found in the mansion and monastery, as well as key documents that told the story of the secrets unveiled. The security team had been trained to ensure the protection of the valuable items on display and the safety of visitors.

Emily was in the conference room, preparing for a special presentation she was going to give during the opening. His speech was to address not only the historical aspects of the Whitmore family, but also the broader issues of the influence of shadows on history and the importance of research and knowledge.

Dr. Carter was in the library, reviewing the last details of the archives that were to be made available to researchers and visitors. He had worked tirelessly to ensure that all information was accurate and accessible.

Opening day arrived, and the Whitmore Mansion was filled with visitors, scholars, and members of the local community. Lisa, Daniel, Emily, and Dr. Carter were at the entrance, greeting guests and guiding them through the new facility.

The ceremony began with a keynote address by Dr. Carter, who thanked everyone for their support and highlighted the purpose of the research center. He mentioned the team's hard work and commitment to transforming the Whitmore family's dark past into a lesson in learning and reflection.

Then, Emily took the stage for her performance. His speech was applauded by the audience, and his ability to connect the story to broader issues left a lasting impression on everyone present. He spoke about how confronting the dark aspects of history not only reveals the truth, but also offers the opportunity to build a brighter, more conscious future.

During the event, Daniel and Lisa met with several people interested in collaborating with the research center. There were researchers, historians, and scholars who were eager to contribute to the center's mission and further explore issues related to the Whitmore family.

The opening was a resounding success, and the Whitmore Mansion began to receive visitors from all over the world. Exhibitions and lectures offered in-depth and educational insight into the history and secrets of the family, and the center established itself as a reference place for the study of historical and esoteric subjects.

As night fell and the event drew to a close, Lisa, Daniel, Emily, and Dr. Carter found themselves in the mansion's garden, enjoying a quiet moment after the busy day. The view of the illuminated building and the joyful bustle of visitors reminded them of the positive impact of their work.

"I think we've accomplished something really important," Lisa said, as she looked at the building with a satisfied smile. "What began as a dark mystery has become a source of knowledge and reflection."

Daniel nodded, looking around. "Yes, and the center not only preserves history, but also reminds us of the importance of facing our fears and learning from our past."

Emily, with a contemplative smile, added, "Our work has shown that even the darkest chapters can be transformed into opportunities for learning and understanding."

Dr. Carter, with typical serenity, concluded, "The Whitmore family's story has been revealed and understood, and the legacy of the research center will live on to educate and warn future generations."

The group was silent for a moment, absorbing the meaning of their achievements. The Whitmore mansion, once a symbol of dark secrets, now stood as a beacon of light and knowledge. They had faced challenges, unraveled mysteries, and in the end, had turned a shadow story into a testament to resilience and redemption.

With one last look at the mansion and a sense of fulfillment, Lisa, Daniel, Emily, and Dr. Carter prepared to close the chapter of their own story. They knew that the research center would continue to grow and evolve, and they were proud to have played a role in transforming the Whitmore family's legacy into a source of inspiration and learning for all.

Milton Keynes UK
Ingram Content Group UK Ltd.
UKHW051705221024
449870UK00012B/72

9 798227 898760